Judith Resnik

Challenger
Astronaut

USA
NASA
Challenger

Judith Resnik

Challenger Astronaut

Joanne E. Bernstein and Rose Blue
with Alan Jay Gerber

Lodestar Books
Dutton New York

Library of Congress Cataloging-in-Publication Data

Bernstein, Joanne E.
Judith Resnik, Challenger astronaut / Joanne Bernstein and Rose Blue with Alan Jay Gerber.
p. cm.
Includes bibliographical references.
Summary: A biography of the astronaut; a woman, a doctor of electrical engineering, and a Jew; who was killed in the explosion of the space shuttle Challenger.
ISBN 0-525-67305-9
1. Resnik, Judith, 1949–1986—Juvenile literature. 2. Astronauts—United States—Biography—Juvenile literature. 3. Challenger (Spacecraft)—Accidents—Juvenile literature. [1. Resnik, Judith, 1949–1986. 2. Astronauts. 3. Jews—Biography. 4. Challenger (Spacecraft—Accidents.) I. Blue, Rose. II. Gerber, Alan Jay. III. Title. IV. Series.
TL789.85.R52B47 1990
629.45'092—dc20 89-13355
[B] CIP
[92] AC

Published in the United States by Lodestar Books, an affiliate of Dutton Children's Books, a division of Penguin Books USA Inc.

Published simultaneously in Canada by Fitzhenry & Whiteside Limited, Toronto

Editor: Virginia Buckley

Design by Stanley S. Drate/Folio Graphics Co. Inc.

Printed in the U.S.A. First Edition 10 9 8 7 6 5 4 3 2 1

in memory of
Dr. Judith A. Resnik,
successor to Jewish pioneers
and explorers through the ages

CONTENTS

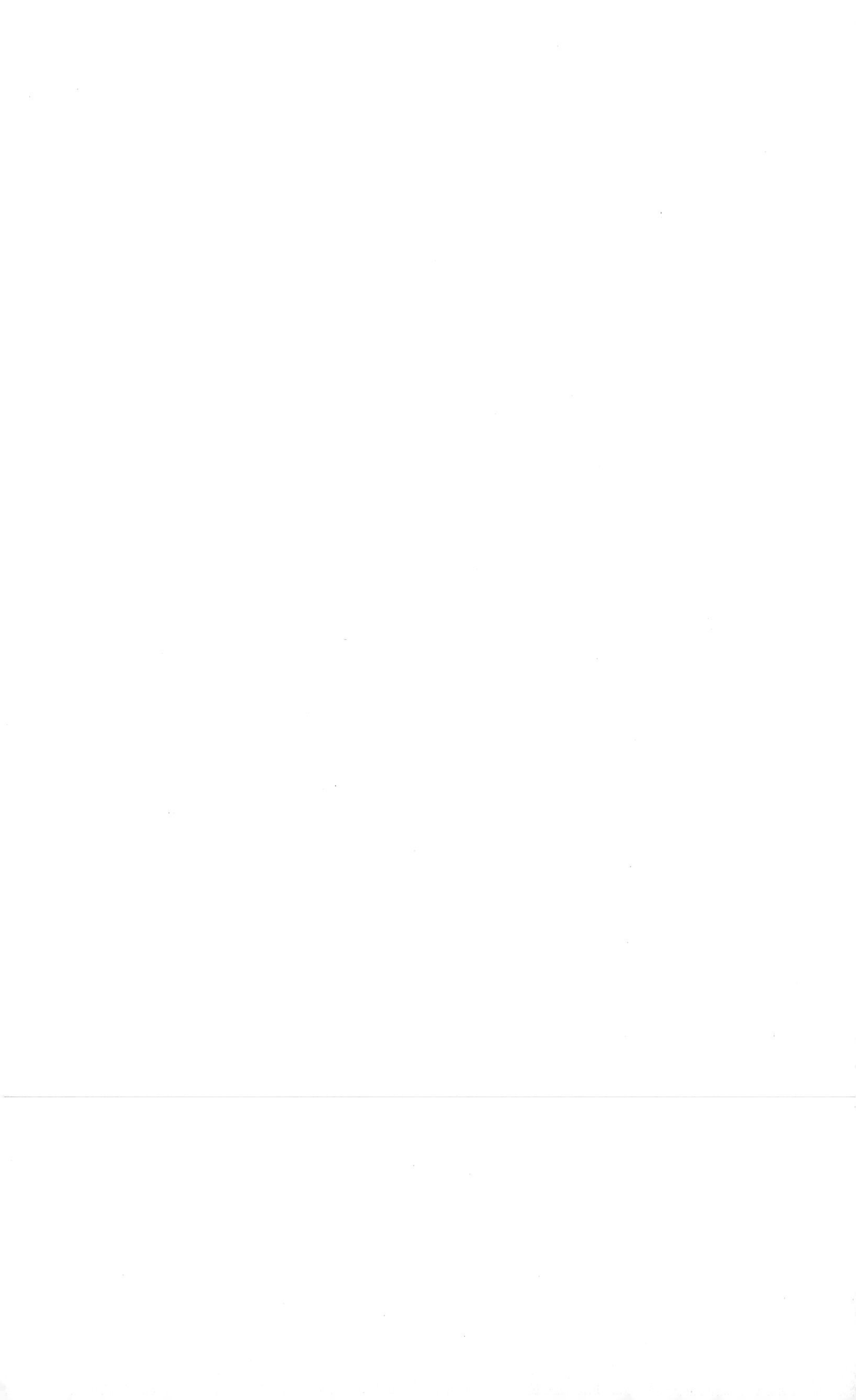

REACHING FOR THE STARS

They slipped the surly bonds of earth to touch the face of God.

—President Ronald Reagan
in a tribute to the Challenger crew

On the morning of January 28, 1986, astronaut Judith A. Resnik of Akron, Ohio, was killed in the fiery explosion of the space shuttle Challenger. She was thirty-six years old, a doctor of electrical engineering, and an American Jew.

Judith Resnik was embarking on her second mission into space. An intensely private person, she shunned the publicity that usually envelops the elite members of the space shuttle flights. The fanfare went to another woman in the Challenger crew. And this was so even in death, when the public's attention focused first on schoolteacher Christa McAuliffe.

Judith Resnik was a scientist who loved her work and gave her life for it. Her work was reaching for the stars. This is her story.

Judith Resnik

Challenger
Astronaut

1

Changing Course Forever

No woman should be denied anything by accident of gender, including the right to risk death.

—Pete Hamill, writing about the Challenger disaster

"T minus forty-five seconds and counting." It is Tuesday, January 28, 1986, coming up on 11:38 in the morning. The countdown is under way. On the launch platform at the Kennedy Space Center in Cape Canaveral, Florida, the space shuttle Challenger stands poised and waiting for its long-awaited ascent.

Originally scheduled for January 20, the lift-off date was changed to Saturday, January 25, because one of the other space shuttles, the Columbia, had been delayed. When January 25 arrived, a dust storm was brewing in Senegal, an African country at the other end of the world. Under stringent National Aeronautics and Space Administration (NASA) safety rules, a shuttle cannot fly unless there is a safe place for an emergency landing if something is amiss before the craft goes into orbit. That faraway dust storm was cause enough to delay the launch one more day.

On January 26, the weather was uncooperative. A cold front was blustering down the Florida peninsula, rain showers heralding its arrival. Because of the great speeds space vehicles reach immediately after lift-off, rain can damage the heat-resistant tiles that protect the shuttle's thin outer covering. The Challenger could not go up in rain, not even a slight drizzle.

Monday, January 27, arrived and seemed more promising. Once again the crew of the Challenger strapped themselves in place, ready to go. From her reclining seat on the upper deck, Judith Resnik could glimpse the vibrant expanse of blue sky. Soon she would fly into that wonderful sky.

The countdown began, getting as far as T (takeoff) minus nine minutes. Then the countdown stopped and remained at that point for four hours. This delay became an embarrassment to the NASA. One bumble followed another. The ground crew tried to remove a hatch handle on the outside of the spacecraft but couldn't. A bolt was stuck. Technicians called for a special drill. It took twenty minutes to arrive, but the drill's battery was dead. Although the space program has a multi-billion dollar budget, another such drill didn't seem to be available. The technicians tried for an hour and a half and finally loosened the bolt with a simple hacksaw.

While they worked, the weather had changed. Winds as strong as thirty-five miles per hour gusted across the launch platform. Such high winds are too strong for a return landing if a malfunction occurs immediately after lift-off. Faces reddened over their inept performances and, frustrated by the tricky weather, officials scrubbed the flight, rescheduling it for the next day.

On Tuesday, January 28, it is not raining. The wind has died down. The sky is clear, but it is an unseasonably cold

Florida day. The night before, the temperature plunged to twenty-seven degrees Fahrenheit. By daybreak it reached just above freezing. Now, almost mid morning, the temperature has risen a few more degrees. The cold weather can damage rubber rings in the rocket boosters, which keep burning fuel from leaking. Icicles hang from the spacecraft and launch platform. Like rain, icicles can damage the heat-shield tiles.

NASA officials inspect the site and decide the rocket booster ring seals will be all right. They decide the ice will not create a problem, either. They consult with top administrators at Morton Thiokol, the manufacturer of the seals, who, against the advice of their engineers, say the flight is safe. But they put off launch time for two hours to reinspect the icicles. An engineer from Rockwell, the company that built the Challenger, watching from California on closed-circuit television, calls the Kennedy Space Center to advise delaying the flight because of the icicles. But the Space Center director, heeding others' contrary advice that little risk exists, orders the countdown to continue.

To everyone's great relief, the countdown matches and then surpasses the aborted countdown of the day before. Bundled in sweaters and jackets, shivering family members, spectators, and reporters cheer when the voice on the loudspeaker announces, "We're at nine minutes and counting." Soon the words are, "We're at eight minutes and counting."

The minutes and seconds tick by. Inside the orbiter, Challenger crew members check and recheck the indicators on their elaborate machinery. The main computer, backed up by four others, gives continuous information from 2,000 sensors and data points. Everything seems just fine. The walkway is removed from Challenger.

"T minus four minutes and counting." The temperature is thirty-eight degrees. Mission Control tells the crew to ready their helmets for flight by closing the visors, which are air-tight.

The announcer starts counting down in smaller intervals. "T minus two minutes and twenty seconds. No unexpected errors reported."

Is Challenger finally going to take off? After all these delays, will it really happen?

"Ninety seconds and counting. The 51-L mission ready to go."

"T minus forty-five seconds and counting."

"T minus ten . . . nine . . . eight . . . seven . . . six . . . We have main engine start."

"Three . . . two . . . one . . . And lift-off."

Hundreds of spectators cheer as they feel the power of the controlled ignition explosion that sends the Challenger thundering out of the billowing smoke like a huge, graceful white bird ascending into the crisp blue Florida sky.

Few people realize the courage needed to sit on the end of a candle that is about the same size as a 727 jet, hitched up to hundreds of thousands of gallons of liquid hydrogen and oxygen, and more than two million pounds of solid fuel—and then have someone light the match! Probably most people in such a situation would be frightened to death. But astronaut Judith Resnik doesn't regard her job that way. She doesn't look upon herself as brave, and she doesn't regard her career as frightening. She knows, of course, the dangers of space travel, but she feels that something is dangerous only, in her words, "if you are not prepared for it, . . . or if you can't think through how to get yourself out of a problem." And Judith Resnik has prepared for this day for nearly eight years.

"Houston, we have roll program," comes word from the Challenger. "Roger, roll Challenger" is the reply from Mission Control. Sixteen seconds into flight 51-L, the white space bird arches gracefully over on its back, and external fuel tank and rocket boosters are now in the proper position for orbit entry.

"Challenger, go with throttle up." Fifty-two seconds into flight 51-L. The engines of the great white bird have now reached full power. Mission Control informs the crew that the greatest stress on the space shuttle as it blasts upward is now beginning.

Judith and the rest of the Challenger crew are prepared for the stress. Space training is a long, methodical process that is both tedious and exciting. Astronauts know that the launch phase of any mission is the most difficult and dangerous time. But with their heads rattling inside their space helmets, Judith and the others can barely hear the steady voice of Mission Control in their headsets. The engines thunder and the rockets scream. And the Challenger keeps climbing. There is no time for fright, no time to think of danger. At this point in the flight, the situation is out of the crew's control. On a flight of several days' duration the only time that a spacecraft is controlled by technology and not by its astronauts is immediately after launch. Judith once said that the one time space flight could be dangerous is "if you don't have control over it." These first moments are such a time.

Sixty seconds after takeoff, shuttle flight 51-L is eight miles above ground. The spacecraft is traveling at the amazing speed of just under 2,000 miles per hour.

And then, suddenly, a flicker of orange dances just past the center of the spacecraft. Then a bigger flare, reaching out, reaching upward. All of this in the barest of milliseconds. And then fire fills the sky. Tongues of orange, red, and yellow shoot out from a great puffy white cloud like a space monster devouring its prey. The booster snakes crazily out of control. One minute and thirteen seconds, and it is all over. Not everyone realizes it yet, but it is over. The space mission is gone, the crew of the space shuttle is gone, and the bright future of Challenger astronaut Dr. Judith Resnik is gone.

Later, Dr. Marvin Resnik, Judith's grieving father, recalled the pattern of smoke visible from the disintegrating spacecraft. It seemed to Dr. Resnik to form the letter Y, representing his anguish. Many, many times since that day, he has asked himself and others the unanswerable question, the question he asked the day the future died. Why?

2

The Young Judy

Daddy, this is Little.

—Judith Resnik, to her father

Who was Judith Resnik? She was an astronaut. She was a woman. She was a Jew. But before she became an astronaut, she was a child, a daughter, a schoolgirl.

Judith Arlene Resnik was born in Akron, Ohio, on April 5, 1949. April is considered the month of Jewish pioneers. It was in April 1654 that the first Jewish colonists made their way to the shores of Nieuw Amsterdam, now New York. And it was in April 1909 that the city of Tel Aviv was founded by the *chalutzim*, pioneers from Europe who settled in what was then Palestine.

From the moment Judy was born, her parents fed her information, heartily stuffed her with concepts that would enhance whatever aptitude for high achievement she already possessed. And she loved every moment of learning: Throw her a new vocabulary word, toss her a science question, and Judy ate it up like food. By the time Judy entered kindergarten, she could already read and do math. Her teacher wanted to skip her into first grade. After consultation with the school psychologist and Judy's parents, the decision was made: She could handle the challenge; she went into first grade. From the start, she was a standout.

And it wasn't easy to stand out in Judy's family, either, for everyone strove to be smart. Judy's cousin Helene says, "If you're looking for family traits, you'd have to say there is a big study ethic. The family has a lot of what you might call overachievers, people who are highly competitive."

When Judy was small, every Friday evening she and her extended family gathered together in Cleveland, thirty miles from Akron, for a dinner to welcome in the Sabbath. Every Friday it was the same. A noisy crowd of adults and children, enough to fill two large tables—the grown-ups at one, the children at the other—flocked into Judy's grandparents' home.

Judy's paternal grandparents, Jacob and Anna, officiated over the meal. Every Friday evening, Jacob, a rabbi and cantor, led the kiddush over wine and challah, the twisted egg bread traditional for Sabbath meals. Every Friday evening Judy's Bubbie (grandmother) Anna lit and blessed the Sabbath candles, a tradition called *bentch licht* in Yiddish. And every Friday evening, Bubbie Anna served the meal she had happily cooked for this multitude of hers. The menu never changed: gefilte fish for a first appetizer, followed by homemade chicken soup with the thinnest of noodles floating in it as a second appetizer. After that came the main course, roast chicken, with potatoes as a side dish.

The meal was always the same, the group was always the same, the activities were always the same. There was lots of happy singing—the traditional *zemiroth*. Both Rabbi Jacob and Judy's father had training as cantors and many others in the group had good singing voices. Besides singing, the other main activity was conversation and, like the blessings, meal, and lusty singing, the weekly conversation was essentially the same: What was new in the family, and more pointedly, what were the latest accomplishments of the various family members?

The tradition of accomplishment and risk was a long one. As a rabbi, Jacob had studied the Torah, Talmud, and other learned works for many years. His work was not in a pulpit, but as a ritual slaughterer of kosher meat, the person who gives sanction to a meat processing plant to kill the animal in ways designated to be kosher. In fact, the family name Resnik in Russian means butcher, and the license to sanction and perform *shechitah* (ritual slaughter) is a high honor in Judaism.

Rabbi Jacob and his wife, Anna, took a mutual risk when, in the late 1920s, they moved with their children from Kiev, Russia, to Palestine (now Israel). Some of the children, including Judy's father, Marvin, received much of their education in Palestine. Marvin learned Hebrew and studied the Bible and other works critical to Jewish thought at the Hebron Yeshiva. Hebron is considered one of the holiest cities, second only to Jerusalem. However, shortly after the Hebron massacres in 1929, the Resniks moved to the United States.

The union of Jacob and Anna produced six children, all of whom achieved in accordance with the American ethic of seeking advanced schooling and making a good living. Their son Albert became a dentist, Joseph ran a vending machine business, Dave was a pawnbroker, Shirley taught piano and ran an advertising business, and Harold and Marvin were both optometrists.

Into this heady Sabbath dinner crew were born Judy, her younger brother Charles, and her many cousins. Although Judy was a private person even at a young age, father and daughter were close. He taught Judy to enjoy a job well done and he watched proudly as she showed early signs of intellectual promise. In first grade, his little Judy was already reading at third-grade level. Marvin Resnik engaged Judy's innate curiosity by teaching her to be unafraid of the physical world. With her father, Judy learned the pleasures of doing electrical repairs and building simple machines. Along with his instruction, Marvin brought basic joys to his daughter—ice cream, humor, a buoyant spirit with which to share the many steps of growing up.

Marvin never told people the cute things Chuck and Judy did when they were kids, only how smart they were. Somehow, though, even if Marvin stressed being smart over other qualities, his way of doing it didn't seem a strain, and Judy always looked to him for love and guidance.

Mother and daughter were not as close. Sarah Resnik, formerly a legal secretary, tried to teach Judy, too, instructing her not in science but in the things she knew and valued. She taught Judy how to cook and provided lessons in piano and, later, in typing and shorthand. But Sarah's teaching didn't result in the same closeness Judy had with her father. Sarah Resnik believed in busy, strict schedules, unrelieved by jokes or sweets. From rigorous expectations came a sense of worth, Sarah Resnik believed.

Perhaps mother and daughter were too much alike in some ways. Both were strong-willed and determined to succeed in their pursuits. Sarah Resnik felt that Judy and her younger brother Charles would benefit from learning the value of discipline and organization. Judy did learn to be neat and to pay attention to details, but she also learned resentment, a resentment that would grow and smother any love that had existed between mother and daughter.

In whatever she did, Judy strove for high achievement. She so impressed a teacher that she skipped into first grade at Fairlawn Elementary School. She also impressed every teacher at the Temple Beth El Sunday School, where she was instructed in Hebrew and Jewish culture. She skipped a grade in Hebrew school, too. Bea Pollack, Judy's first-grade Sunday school teacher, found Judy a joy to have as a pupil. To Mrs. Pollack, Judy was a serious little girl, "more serious than most." She was responsive in class, not mischievous as other children often were. Still, she was sweet, friendly, joyful. She was bright and enthusiastic about Hebrew and good at her work. In Mrs. Pollack's class, Judy learned to light the Sabbath candles. One day she delighted Mrs. Pollack by bringing her father to meet the teacher whom she loved. No wonder Mrs. Pollack found her so lovable she wished she were her mother.

A young Judy Resnik lights the Sabbath eve candles as classmates from her religious school look on. She is covering her eyes, according to Jewish custom.

Through most of the years of Hebrew school, Rena Wish Cohen was one of Judy's classmates. One year, the students were assigned to perform a skit before an audience. Young Rena was to accompany a singer on the piano. Rena's piano skills did not match Judy's and she was very nervous. Judy tried to help and encourage her friend, allaying her fears and giving her confidence. "Don't worry," Judy told Rena. "All you have to do is hit the chords. Just one chord after another." Though Judy was said to be reserved, she often offered such warmth and encouragement.

A winsome pair, Judy and Rena become teachers' pets. The two were the first girls in their temple permitted to read from the Torah on Sabbath morning. Since the traditional laws do not sanction that, the two girls were breaking tradition in their accomplishment.

Judy did well in Hebrew school, and she enjoyed being part of a Jewish circle during her early years. Her father remained active as a part-time cantor, traveling several times a year to a temple in Pennsylvania to help conduct services. Growing up in Palestine, he had retained ties to Hebrew and Yiddish culture. He injected Hebrew words into the life he shared with his daughter. K'tanah was Marvin's nickname for Judy. It means "little one," and soon cousins also called Judy K'tanah. Judy enjoyed the nickname, and signed her letters to her father that way, sometimes in Hebrew, K'tanah, sometimes in English, Little. Adopting her father's affection for the Hebrew language, she frequently addressed him as Abba, the Hebrew term for "father."

The most memorable occasion of Judy's stay in Hebrew school was her Bat Mitzvah, of course. At the time, in 1962, it was customary for males to become Bar Mitzvah, or sons of the covenant, growing into men in the eyes of Judaism. The notion of affording the same rituals and responsibilities to females was a fairly new idea.

Judy's coming of age was heralded in a column on page one of the Temple bulletin: "Our Bat Mitzvah this Friday evening is the daughter of Dr. and Mrs. Marvin Resnik, the granddaughter of the Reverend and Mrs. Jacob Resnik and Mr. and Mrs. Max Polensky of Cleveland Heights; and the great-granddaughter of Mrs. Ida Resnik of Cleveland." The announcement went on to invite the congregation to join in the services to celebrate with the family.

Both rabbis at Temple Beth El helped Judy prepare for her Bat Mitzvah. Rabbi Philip Salzman spoke of her in absolutes: "Judy is the best student I have ever had in Hebrew school." Rabbi Samuel S. Lerer, the senior rabbi, talked with Judy occasionally and found her a bit reserved. As was his custom, he met with the parents prior to the Bat Mitzvah and for the rehearsal. In these meetings, he was under the impression they were "a good, united family." This impression would prove to be wrong.

Judy officiated for part of the Friday evening service on April 6 and chanted the Haftorah, a portion of the Torah. Haftorah readings are chosen in conjunction with the Hebrew calendar, in a repeating cycle. The Haftorah for Judy's Bat Mitzvah day was called Tazriah. As in most Bar and Bat Mitzvoth, the subject of the Haftorah is of less interest to the audience than watching a youngster who has grown up before their eyes take on and master a challenging task.

A large audience attended the service. Judy, dressed in blue and wearing a white choir robe trimmed in black, concluded the service by offering a prayer before the Aron Kodesh, the Holy Ark bearing the Torah scrolls. "She wasn't nervous at all," thought her friend Barbara Cheek. After the services came the Oneg Shabbat, a festive reception to welcome the Sabbath. At this special Oneg Shabbat, friends, relatives, and congregants toasted and celebrated the official entrance into Judaism of the girl in whom they took so much pride.

The qualities Sarah and Marvin Resnik instilled and refined in their daughter served her well at Fairlawn Elementary School and Simon Perkins Junior High School. In many ways Judy was typical, just one of the crowd. Like her friends, she moaned about the fortunes of the nearby Cleveland Indians baseball team. She rolled her wavy dark hair on empty orange juice cans at night, hoping to straighten it out a bit. But she wanted her hair straighter still. To get a satisfactory look, she set an electric iron on low and ironed the curl out of her locks as best she could.

Like many young girls, Judy also enjoyed giggling in a small clique, sharing secrets no one else knew. In junior high, Judy, Barbara Cheek, and Barbara's older sister, Pam, were the Three Musketeers, according to Barbara. The Cheeks lived a half-block from the Resniks, and they had known one another for what seemed like forever. Every morning, Judy waited in front of the Cheeks' house for the school bus to take them off for the day.

The Three Musketeers rode in the bus as a group, ate lunch as a group, and still sought one another out after school, congregating at the Resnik or Cheek house until dinner.

Judy was supportive of Barbara when she needed help. At the start of junior high, Barbara was apprehensive. She had heard that junior high was a place where there were hoods and where you could get into trouble. She was scared. Judy said, "You just stay away from the boys with long hair and Cuban heels. You'll be just fine."

In these ways—trying to achieve a certain look, having a circle of friends and caring for them—Judy was a typical teenager. In many other ways, however, she was not at all typical. Although other youngsters read books, Judy read urgently and avidly, seeking a sense of completion in the task as she dashed through the complete set of Nancy Drew mysteries that her father had brought her. Other girls learned how to make a bed, bake cookies, and iron, but with Judy there was an effort to have everything come out just so. When she went bowling with her father every Sunday, though she never became a good bowler, the tally sheets she kept for them were the straightest in the bowling alley. Her father told others, "She's the neatest scorekeeper in the world." It was the same perfectionist spirit that led Judy to achieve a typing speed of ninety words a minute without a single mistake.

By the time she was a teenager, young Judith Resnik could truly play the piano, being one of a handful of the world's children who didn't have to be forced to practice. When company came over, Judy got up on her own and went to the piano to play for them. As her uncle Joseph said, "They didn't even have to ask." Judy took lessons from two famous Akron musicians, Arthur Reginald and Pat Pace, who helped cultivate a true classical talent. Both felt she had what it took to become a concert pianist.

Sarah had taught her daughter through regimentation, but at times she could empathize as well. When Judy was in junior high, the family dog, Pansy, was hit by a car and killed. Sarah extended herself by calling two of Judy's girlfriends in the neighborhood. She asked them to come over and help Judy through the crisis. Judy cried when she answered the door and brought the girls inside to recite together the Kaddish, the traditional Jewish prayer of mourning.

Such was the legacy of Sarah's upbringing, a mixture of discipline and feeling. Judy showed extraordinary discipline in piano, typing, cooking, but perhaps the thing that most set her apart from other girls during this period was her developing capability in science and math. Although she showed no special interest in the space program at that time, she was fascinated by figures and formulas and conceptual puzzles. As with the vocabulary words her family would toss out to her to play with in earlier days, Judy was able to solve whatever hard examples and problems the teachers had in store. This growing ability would become the mortar for the building blocks of her eventual career.

3

The Growing Years

She learned to put things in the right perspective.

—Joseph Resnik, speaking of his niece as a teenager

Judy's intense concentration allowed her to juggle many activities at once. When Judy entered Harvey S. Firestone High School as a member of the class of 1966, she managed an armload. She maintained top-notch grades, sought further Jewish education, and made her own beginning forays into male-female relationships, all the while enduring parents who were continually at war. Judy's mother and father now fought about nearly everything. Charges flew mercilessly back and forth. Sarah found fault with everything Marvin did. Marvin talked about Sarah as though she were crazy and evil.

In the mornings, Judy would leave for high school, which became a haven from the emotional chaos at home. Firestone is known as the place where people who have money send their kids. The best courses are offered there, and Judy took advantage of the most advanced ones, particularly in science and math. One of Judy's math teachers,

Burton Willeford, saw her as the best student he'd ever taught. "She's at the top end in everything she does," he said.

Donald Nutter, Judy's teacher for solid geometry and calculus, had a more complex picture of Judy, viewing her as "not necessarily a pure mathematician by nature, not overly blessed with great math insight. In order to excel, she would spend time on the task." To him, Judy had a very logical mind, never showed up unprepared, and got "a good thorough understanding of the material." Then, according to Nutter, she could remember it and use it.

The motto of Firestone reads, "We try harder," and Judy certainly did. Her math tests were so good that Mr. Nutter marked her paper first, then used her answers as a key for the entire class.

Nutter saw Judy as a typical teenager, wearing saddle shoes and no makeup to class, and always nicely groomed. "She wouldn't stand out in a hill of beans," he said, "except for her attitude of excellence." Nutter saved Judy's advanced placement test, using it as a model of neatness and logical thinking with many classes to come.

Judy's attitude of excellence stretched to Judaic studies as well. After her Bat Mitzvah, Judy continued to study and was enrolled in classes leading to confirmation. Candidates for confirmation have to learn more Hebrew and gain a deeper knowledge of Jewish history and tradition. The confirmation ceremony is a time for reaffirmation and recommitment to the Jewish faith. What with homework from Firestone and piano practice an hour each day, Judy had little time to prepare for the weekly confirmation classes. She did her work for it on the bus on the way home from school.

Judy's confirmation class was led by Rabbi Lerer and lasted for two years. Judy was one of nineteen students. The preparation course included instruction in Jewish history, religious and moral beliefs, the meaning of Jewish customs and ceremonies, and the value of practicing Judaism in daily life.

The students also discussed personal hopes, dreams, and ambitions. Judy talked about such matters in a highly thoughtful and intelligent manner. Listening to her, Rabbi Lerer felt Judy was a person who would most likely succeed in life.

During this period, America was beginning to expand its space and satellite program, especially following the mounting pressures after Sputnik, the Russians' daring spacecraft that alerted the United States it might be left behind in a crucial race. Judy approached Rabbi Lerer with many questions pertaining to the space program. "What would Judaism say about it? Would Judaism encourage it?" In response, Rabbi Lerer taught the lesson from the Torah that "man was made in the image of God and has been granted dominance over all creation."

After more than two years of study, the congregation of Temple Beth El was notified of the confirmation services in a bulletin that included photographs of the nineteen youngsters, Judy among them. The ceremony took place on Sunday, June 7, 1964, at 7:30 P.M., on the twenty-seventh day of the Hebrew month Sivan, during the year 5724 of the Hebrew calendar.

The ceremony drew nearly all 2,000 members of the congregation. There was a musical cantata at which each student made a presentation. The congregants listened attentively as Judy delivered her speech.

She said:

> Our Holy Torah relates to us that when our forefathers assembled at the foot of Mount Sinai to receive the Ten Commandments, they rejoiced so much that they exclaimed, "Na-ah-seh-ve-nish-mah—We shall do and shall obey." Our forefathers pledged themselves to

> obey even before knowing what was written in the Torah.
>
> All through the ages, we the children of Israel have been saying: "Na-ah-seh-ve-nish-mah"—We shall do and we shall obey. By birth we became the heirs of the Jewish heritage, the Torah. As we are trained to speak our mother tongue, so we are taught to observe Jewish customs and to repeat exalted truths even before our minds are ripe enough to understand them.
>
> In order to permit our heritage to take deep root in our hearts, . . . we must learn to understand [our religion's] beautiful teachings and to become Jews by choice as well as birth. . . . While we have attended the confirmation class of Beth El Congregation, we have learned to understand the history of Israel and to glory in the words of our prophets. Though much remains to be learned about our religion, we have gathered enough knowledge to realize that our faith has been the light of the world, the glory of all nations. We know ours is a priceless heritage.
>
> The world now stands in greatest need of its spirit, to heal all wounds inflicted by greed and hatred, and to guide humanity out of darkness into the Light of God.
>
> At this time, we the confirmants solemnly pledge ourselves to be forever faithful to the God of our fathers. . . . We pledge ourselves to live up to the precepts of Judaism and to labor with all our might in behalf of Israel's cause and for all humanity.

As part of the ceremony, Rabbi Lerer whispered a brief private message to each of those confirmed. He delivered the following charge to Judith Resnik: "March on, forward and upward."

Thus, at the time of year when the Torah was given at Mount Sinai, signaling the contemporary holiday of Shevuoth, Judith Resnik reaffirmed her commitment to Judaism. The confirmation rite of passage was followed by a tremendous reception in celebration. That evening, Judy was justly joyful and proud.

Toward the end of high school, Judy participated in another rite of passage, not a religious one, but a rite of passage nonetheless. Members of her group were now old enough to drive. They had wheels! Judy and her girlfriends cruised around the parking lot of the Skyway Drive-In Restaurant, looking for boys. They drove around until they found cute boys, then parked near them, hoping something would happen.

Most of the boys who hung out at Skyway were students at Copley High School. Judy liked to socialize with the Copley boys because at Firestone she was known as a brain and was termed unapproachable, on a pedestal. The boys at her own school didn't think of her as a girlfriend.

Boys and books were a conflict for Judy, partly because she was attracted to boys who were not her equal as students. At one time, Judy had a crush on a football player. While driving with her friend Brent Sisler, the two spotted her football idol with another girl, in the girl's car. Judy didn't like him hanging out with other girls. She wanted him to be more committed to her. Devastated, she asked Brent to drive her home.

When they got to her house, Judy told Brent that she was going in to study for a test. The event stayed in his mind. Here was a teenage girl studying for a high school exam even though she was heartbroken.

To some, she seemed the model of obedience and compliance, but Judy was a pawn in the war between her parents. Sarah Resnik didn't want Judy to venture out too much. In her high school years, ice skating was a popular pastime, and Judy wanted skates. But her mother said no. Marvin went out and bought her skates. Sarah burned them—and Marvin got her another pair.

Sarah discouraged dating, too. Judy rebelled. There were brief episodes, like the night she sneaked out to meet a boyfriend, Mark Broida. Judy crawled out a back window, went to a movie with Mark, and came back. Nobody even knew that she had been gone.

And there were more enduring rebellions. Perhaps the most intense rebellion centered around a young man named Len Nahmi. Len Nahmi was probably as much Judy's opposite as he could be. She was at the top of her class at Firestone. He was third from the bottom in a rough Akron high school. She was the child of a professional with post-graduate degrees. He was the child of a rubber worker in the Akron factories. She was Jewish, from an exuberantly religious family. He was half Irish and half Lebanese—an Arab, in the eyes of Sarah and Marvin. On their opposition to Len Nahmi, they could agree.

Judy met Len for the first time at a basketball game. She had gone there with a boy who was heir to a chain of formalwear shops—certainly a boy more to the liking of Mr. and Mrs. Resnik. Immediately taken with Judy's charm, Len asked her date, whom he knew, to introduce them.

Judy responded to Len's street smarts and sense of humor. Slight of build and resembling Bob Dylan, Len could command with his eyes, and it soon became clear that he and Judy shared intensity and ambition. Although he was not a good student, Len longed to fly airplanes and knew a great deal about the aeronautic career he wanted to pursue. Judy explained away his low academic ranking in a second-rate school, seeing his performance as a grand rejection of middle-class values.

Len just wouldn't follow the Resnik rules of hard work for success, and he quickly became a source of contention. Marvin and Sarah pressured their daughter to stop dating him, but that only made their laughter-filled, fast rides in Len's dilapidated car all the more intriguing.

Finally Sarah and Marvin told Judy she couldn't see Len anymore. The young people thought up a way to get around the Resniks' prohibition. Len sent his brother Larry to the Resnik home because his brother looked more Jewish than he. Larry introduced himself as Larry Greenberg, and he became a cover for many hours actually spent with Len. In addition, Judy stayed at her cousins' house in Cleveland while she was enrolled in a college course available there to high school students. In Cleveland, too, she met secretly with Len.

During this period of rendezvous with Len, Judy's parents lurched toward the divorce that had been threatening. Although Judy preferred to live with her father, the courts then customarily awarded custody to the mother, and so Sarah was given custody of both children.

Few knew of the turmoil in the Resnik household. Sarah and Marvin's breakup came as a shock to the community. Judy's parents had been longtime members of Temple Beth El, members of the synagogue choir, and personal friends of Rabbi Lerer. Until the end of the marriage, Rabbi Lerer didn't have an inkling of trouble. Rabbi Lerer often spoke of a special affinity he shared with Marvin, as he, too, had been born in Jerusalem. He thought of Marvin as his landsman (person from the same town), and enjoyed the times Marvin sought an opportunity to speak in Hebrew with him. He was dumfounded that in all his discussions with Judy and her parents, he had never detected any family problems of "shalom ba-it" (peace in the home). He was totally amazed to learn that Sarah and Marvin were now divorced.

After the divorce, Judy continued to see Len. If she had hoped that the release from a warring household would ease matters, she found there was little peace to be had. Sarah Resnik still demanded unceasing perfection from her daughter, and her hatred for Len Nahmi became more open. For Judy, the fatigue, frustration, and anger of creating lies in order to see him eventually caused the couple to split.

It was Len who actually ended the romance. Over the telephone from his parents' basement, he told Judy they should stop seeing each other because she was having nothing but anxiety and pain. Judy was wounded, but she did stop seeing him. They were to rendezvous again later, but for now, Judy and Len were no longer a couple.

And so, Judy went back to juggling the different aspects of her life. Marvin Resnik was very proud of his daughter. He always wanted to show her off—her piano playing, her math ability. When he started to brag, she always said, "Oh, Daddy." Judy spoke those two words in the exasperated yet secretly delighted tone youngsters use with proud fathers everywhere.

Sarah's pride in Judy rested elsewhere, in the secretarial skills her daughter was perfecting. Sarah had urged Judy to take shorthand and typing, saying it could be useful to her later on. As with every other endeavor, Judy did very well in shorthand and typing. Sarah was proud Judy was able to land a summer typing job in one of Akron's top-level court-reporting firms. To her mother, Judy was keeping busy and earning what Sarah called mad money.

Judy's high school extracurricular activities included the French and chemistry clubs, and she was elected to the National Honor Society. But the direction in which she was heading was forecast in one picture in the 1966 Firestone High School yearbook, *The Volplane*. It's a picture of the math club. Sitting and standing around a table are fourteen boys, and Judy.

At high school graduation, Judy was valedictorian and one of only four students in her graduating class to wear gold cords on their mortarboards. This meant they had averages of 4 points or better, solid A; Judy's was 4.2, more like A-plus. She was also entering college with one of the best College Board scores imaginable—straight 800s on the tests, a record achieved by only about nine people in the nation each year.

Before leaving for college, Judy took care of an important matter. After a year of living with her mother, Judy went to the local domestic court and asked that her father be given custody. She won her case.

4

College and Beyond

> I think I'm where I am because I just happened to make the right decisions at the times when the decisions were presented to me.
>
> —*Judith Resnik*

With the years at Firestone High coming to an end, Judy had to make some decisions. She considered, more or less seriously, a career as a classical pianist. In fact, her music teachers urged her in that direction. But Judy Resnik was, and always had been, in love with science. She talked over her choices with her father and decided to take a road that, in 1966, was not a well-traveled one for young women. She would study math and science.

Judy had her pick of colleges throughout the country, but she chose Carnegie-Mellon University in Pittsburgh, then known as Carnegie Tech, a school noted for its excellence in the sciences. One of the few female students in the entering freshman class, Judy selected math as her major. She did well in math, but after meeting a young man majoring in electrical engineering, Michael Oldak, she discovered how interesting the practical applications of science could be. She visited some of his engineering classes and soon changed her major to electrical engineering as well.

Judy began to date Michael Oldak; he became the only man she saw seriously during college. Unlike Len Nahmi, Michael was a good student. Unlike Len, he was gregarious, having joined a fraternity on campus. And, finally, unlike Len, Michael was Jewish.

Judy was comfortable with Michael. Like her, he was serious and striving. The two walked around campus happily, often accompanied by a large dog named Elissa. Judy brought Michael home with her to Akron now and then. They stayed at her father's house. On these trips, Judy also somehow fit in some time with Len.

Meantime, there was now a new cast of characters in her father's home. Marvin had remarried. His wife, Betty, was the aunt of Judy's friend Barbara Cheek Roduner. With this marriage, Judy now had a new connection with her close friend; the marriage made them cousins as well. Judy also got to know Betty's identical twin daughters, Linda and Sandy, nine years older than Judy. The three young women became close.

In college, Judy stayed with a small group of friends, some of whom came from her sorority, Alpha Epsilon Phi. She became musical director for her sorority sisters, and oversaw any melodies or songs that were needed for shows or competitions.

Judy was active in the engineering department, too, serving on the advisory committee that helped younger students adjust to college life. The head of the engineering department, Angel Jordan, noted that she was sharp, very articulate, but she didn't want to attract attention. He felt that she had a unique combination of brilliance and concern for others. Although she shared her thoughts only with a select few and went quietly about her business, Judy consented to run for homecoming queen. She was elected runner-up.

Judy's switch from math to engineering was a good choice. At graduation, she was one of the top five students in her field. Judy was headed into the larger world with an honors degree in hand and a fiancé on her arm.

The engagement to Michael was a natural, if unexciting continuation of their exclusive dating. It came about as did many things with Judy—quietly. Michael didn't propose. Neither did Judy. Instead, one day, Judy and Michael were sitting around imagining what they would do after graduation. The thought occurred to one of them that it would be easier if they got married. The other simply agreed.

While plans for the marriage were quiet and calm, there was continuing turmoil between Judy's parents and between Judy and Sarah. Judy had recently sued her mother to obtain the Bat Mitzvah money Sarah was holding in trust for her. And Marvin and Sarah still had nothing but bitter words for each other. In light of all this, two sets of wedding invitations were sent out. The one going to Dr. Resnik's associates read, "daughter of Dr. Marvin Resnik." The one sent to Sarah's family and friends stated that Judy was her daughter.

One month after graduation, the fighting stopped for a happy occasion. On July 14, 1970, Judy and Michael were married at Temple Beth El in Akron. Rabbi Lerer had moved by that time, and the traditional Jewish marriage ceremony was performed by Rabbi Abraham Feffer. The bride wore white lace. The groom wore a tuxedo.

Judy and Michael moved to New Jersey, and they both started engineering jobs with RCA in Moorestown, ten miles from Philadelphia. Judy became part of the missile and surface radar division. Her work included space-related projects, developing circuit design for radar-controlled systems.

Judy and Michael rented an apartment, picked out furniture together, and splurged on a Steinway upright piano with their wedding money. Still going along on the same track, both Judy and Michael registered for evening master's degree courses at the University of Pennsylvania.

Then Michael took the first steps away from the mutual path he and Judy had worked out for themselves. He left engineering. Law was his interest now. In 1971, Michael applied for law school and was accepted at Georgetown University, in the nation's capital. Judy and Michael moved to Washington, D.C.

Judy continued with RCA, transferring to a Springfield, Virginia, office. She finished up her master's at the University of Maryland, and began the next step, a doctoral program. During her studies for a Ph.D., Judy switched jobs. In 1974, she started work as a biomedical engineer at the neurophysiology laboratory at the National Institutes of Health. Here she was able to bring the skills of an engineer to bear on medicine. She also expressed her closeness to her father by choosing optical research. Judy became involved in the study of the effects of electrical currents on the retina, the eye's image detector.

On the surface, all appeared smooth. Judy and Michael bought furniture, and both were studying, going somewhere. Their private lives, though, were marked by dissatisfaction.

In 1975, Judy and Michael separated. Like their engagement and marriage, it was comfortable and quiet. A close friend of Dr. Resnik's, Connie Knapp, said, "They wanted different things in life. He wanted children desperately, and she didn't." Judy's father felt that Judy was probably married to her career.

Judy and Michael remained friends after the marriage dissolved. (For a while, she telephoned Michael nightly, and then the two fell into a pattern of exchanging news every few weeks or so. Michael also remains friends with Dr. Marvin Resnik and represents Judy's estate.)

Judy never told her father why her marriage ended in divorce. There were probably a number of reasons. Partly it might have been Michael's desire for a family. Partly it might have been Judy's desire to concentrate on her doctorate. Perhaps it was time to seek different challenges, different pleasures.

Judy sent Len Nahmi a card. It said, "I'm single."

5
The NASA Challenge

She became a different person. She loves it there. Now she is with people who are all bright, all achievers like herself.

—Betty Resnik about her stepdaughter's acceptance by NASA

Judy had once asked Rabbi Lerer about Judaism's response to space exploration, but she had never expressed any interest in becoming part of the adventure. Up until now, she hadn't been interested in airplanes or astronomy. She didn't like science fiction. She was interested in watching the landing on the moon in July 1969, but so was just about every other American.

What led Judy Resnik to join the space program?

The year was 1977, and her studies were winding up. According to her father, Judy's interest in the space program was piqued when she saw a notice on a bulletin board at work announcing NASA's campaign to recruit new astronauts. Perhaps this could be a logical next step.

Over the years, Judy discussed nearly all important plans with her father. He helped her make many decisions. Dr. Resnik said, "We were very close. I was always consulted."

Judy went to her father. "I'm going to try to be an astronaut," she told him.

"You're going to make it," he replied.

When Len Nahmi received Judy's "I'm single" postcard, he was the one already involved with flying. He was living in Toronto, employed as a pilot for Air Canada. Len quickly made arrangements to fly to Washington to be with Judy. Within days, after more than four years apart, Judy and Len were together once more. It was as though they had never been separated.

Len was able to visit Judy frequently and, like her father, he, too, was interested in her career. Len heard an announcement on the radio that NASA was actively going to recruit minorities and women. His first response was that this might be an opportunity for Judy.

However the idea came to Judy, once it did, she approached the project with typical thoroughness.

After the call for women and minorities went out, NASA received applications from more than 1,000 women. Talented as she was, smart as she was, what chance did she have out of that number?

Judy decided to shorten the odds. She launched an all-out campaign to get herself accepted. To shape up her body, she began a stringent routine of diet and exercise. To become knowledgeable about flying, she studied for a pilot's license. Len encouraged her every step of the way, sending her flight manuals. She got the pilot's certificate swiftly, scoring two 100s and a 98 on the exams. Together Len and Judy pored through former astronaut Michael Collins's book, *Carrying the Fire*. In his book, Collins, who had kept Apollo II in orbit while his fellow crew members made their historic landing on the moon, offered a gold mine of hints on how to be chosen, even revealing how applicants should dress for interviews.

The campaign became a personal promotion effort for

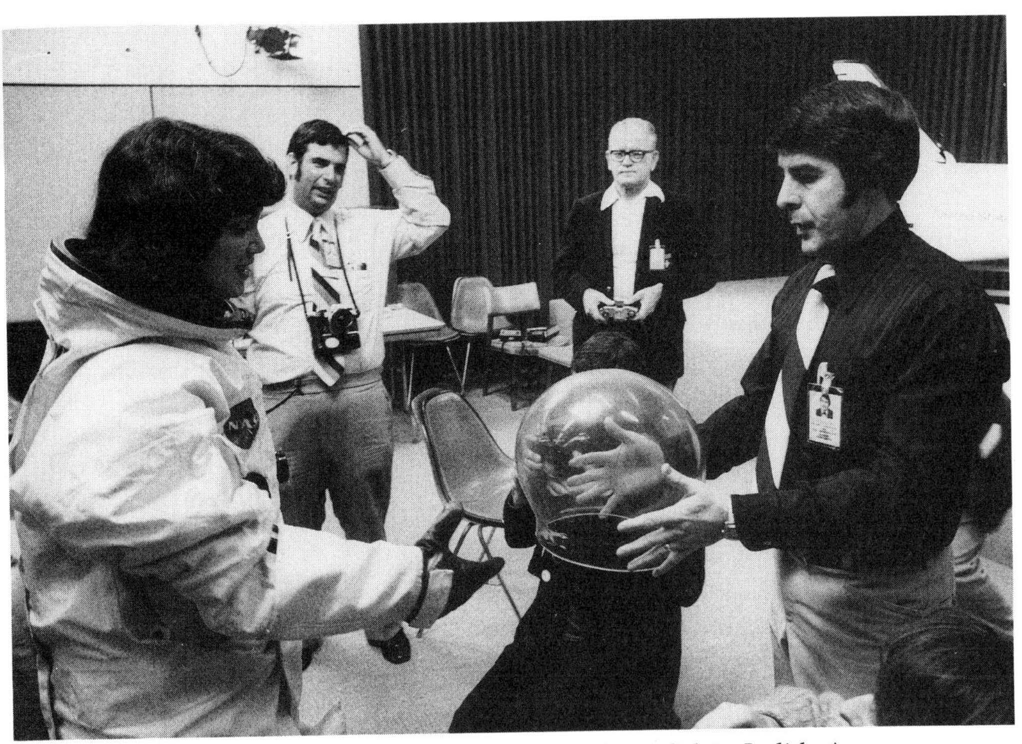

Photographers take pictures as astronaut candidate Judith A. Resnik tries on an extravehicular mobility spacesuit. NASA

both of them. Len figured out how to find Collins's office in the National Air and Space Museum, where Collins now worked as an administrator. Judy strode right up to the ex-astronaut's office and brashly introduced herself. "Hi, Mike, how are you? My name's Judy Resnik, and I want to be an astronaut."

She also tracked down a fellow Ohioan, Senator John Glenn. She asked Glenn, the first American astronaut to orbit the earth, what he thought NASA was seeking in their new recruits. She even cut her mass of dark curly hair, feeling that short locks gave her a more professional look.

Len was accomplished in striving to push himself forward and taught Judy his methods. With the pure gumption Judy had detected even in high school, Len had grown enormously. He had become a flight instructor even before he was a full-fledged adult. To get a license to fly commercially, he had rapidly gone through the University of Akron to pick up the necessary degree. He knew how to make things happen, and he shared his tricks with Judy.

Len told her that whatever good news she received after applying to NASA, she should share with them. If she got a promotion at the National Institutes of Health, she should tell them. When her doctoral degree came through, she should tell them. An academic honor? Tell them that, too, Len advised. And don't tell them in a letter. Tell them in a telegram. Make them sit up and take notice.

After completing work for her doctorate, Judy landed a job with Xerox as a senior systems engineer in product development. She was asked to work in the Los Angeles area. Judy loved the sun. She loved getting tan. Best of all, the California climate was even better for workouts for the NASA tryouts. Judy rented an apartment in Redondo Beach; the beach was nearby. She jogged along the shore, building stamina and cutting down her weight. When her regimen was over, she and Len, still a frequent visitor and ever a coach, would prepare a hearty meal together. Often it was steak and Judy was known to finish off a whole pound of beef after her workout.

The waiting period was difficult for Judy. She was nervous and anxious, concerned she might not be accepted. Said her friend, Barbara Cheek Roduner, "Judy was used to choosing, not being chosen."

Judy worried. She worried about her weight, so she ran more. She worried about her blood pressure, so she had it checked all the time. And she watched what she ate, passing up the sweets she liked in favor of proteins.

The fledgling NASA astronaut NASA

Astronaut training required that Judith practice parachuting to safety (above) and emergency sea landings (right). NASA

Finally, the preparation began to pay off. Judy passed the rigorous NASA physical, and she went through the interviews successfully. First she learned she was one of the top 200 female candidates; then there was more waiting and more worrying. At last, in January 1978, Judith Resnik, along with four women, was accepted by NASA as one of the new astronaut candidates.

She was so happy, she called everyone she knew. Many received the call at six in the morning.

Judith Resnik, Ph.D., newly minted NASA astronaut, was just short of twenty-nine years old. Perhaps because an astronaut's job seems so glamorous and exciting, people rarely talk about how much they get paid! Judy actually had to take a cut in salary to join NASA. As an astronaut she would eventually be paid $42,500 a year, less than she could have earned in industry.

So Judy left Xerox and the promise of high money and success in engineering for the challenge of NASA and space. At the time, her father said, "I think she feels NASA is where she belongs." Later, he would comment, "She was looking for a purpose in life."

Along with the other new candidates, Judy reported to the Johnson Space Center in Houston, Texas, to begin a period of training and evaluation. She relaxed in the disciplined atmosphere of Houston. NASA is a place where you are judged by your work, where everyone is striving for the same goals, where passion and intensity are directed toward the end product—successful flight. There was little place for swapping life histories here, for discussing nagging family problems, for expressing deep feelings. Judy thrived on it.

In NASA, the days were so busy, Judy could leave behind the ragged edges of her relationship with her mother, she could leave behind her anger, she could develop a new identity. She even picked up a new nickname, J.R., and it

Judith learns to control and contain fires. NASA

stuck for the duration. She began to date other astronauts, too. She continued to see Len Nahmi, although he didn't move to Houston. But in a sense, Judy and Len were already separated by her devotion to the space program, a devotion he had intensified.

Judy did very little public relations as an astronaut, although, actually, public relations are a very important job function for astronauts. There are so few scheduled flights that astronauts often wait not months but years to get up into space. Some never do. Once the astronaut's training for a specific role in space is completed, the days must be filled with other activities. Astronauts take turns visiting school assemblies and other community events, explaining the mission of the space program and generating interest and support.

Judy did not enjoy that part of the job very much. She hated television interviews and seldom gave them. She felt that newspaper interviews became too personal. She resented what she regarded as intrusions into her personal life, such as a discussion of her divorce from Michael Oldak. And Judy didn't want to be known as a Jewish astronaut. Or a woman astronaut. She wanted to be just an astronaut.

In response to requests by Jewish organizations and publications, Judy waffled. At times, she declined, because the group had set her aside as a "first." Other times, she consented to an interview or appearance. One year, she appeared at a Jewish Heritage Day at Kiamesha Lake, in New York State, representing science careers. She spoke with pride of being Jewish to the audience of youngsters from nearby camps, many of whom were underprivileged. "There are no bars—no bars to where you can go," she said.

When Judy did get away on vacation, she quietly visited her father and stepmother in Ohio.

Although Judy was uncomfortable about making public appearances before the press and strangers, she was most gracious concerning her longtime friends. Brent Sisler clearly recalled the twelfth reunion of the 1966 graduating class of Firestone High.

"We were only the second class to come out of Firestone," says Brent. "We were college prep. A lot was expected of us."

By the time the twelfth reunion took place, many had fulfilled those expectations. Present were doctors, politicians, engineers, and others with blossoming careers.

Astronaut candidate Resnik is briefed by fellow candidate Michael Coats on the T-38 training plane. NASA

Later, the two take the T-38 up for a brief flight. NASA

The year was 1978, the same year in which Firestone alumna Judith Resnik was accepted into NASA—the year one of the members of the class of '66 had become an astronaut. Judy had kept in touch with a few classmates and had returned to see some teachers, too. Over the years, she had spoken and corresponded with Donald Nutter. When she became an astronaut, he had written to her, saying, "With success on your next mission I greet you." She responded with an autographed picture, which he hung on Firestone High School's Wall of Fame.

The night of the reunion, the question on everyone's lips was, "Is Judy coming? Is Judy coming?" The friends mixed, mingled, and exchanged memories in Nanthe's Restaurant in Akron. Still Judy had not arrived.

Halfway through the evening, nobody had seen Judy. Then as Brent stood chatting with a group of old classmates, he heard a shy, quiet voice say, "Hello, Brent." It was Judy. Brent turned to her and his face lit up.

Judy and Brent had a lovely visit, talking over old times and new. Judy was as friendly as ever. She circulated among the group. Everyone was very impressed that she had chosen to come.

Judy returned to NASA and her training continued. It was still possible that she would be the first woman in space, and she was trained to use a mechanical arm, also called a robot arm. This eventually became her job as a mission specialist. The huge, unwieldy apparatus performs tasks outside the space shuttle but it is operated from inside. To be good at handling it, you have to make the mechanical arm part of your own body and you have to have a very sensitive touch.

J.R. loved the training period. She was not bothered by the long hours she put in improving her capability on the mechanical arm. She could concentrate intently and feel safe in focusing on achievement. Lynn Harvey, a former

Judith, second from left, learns how the control and guidance center works. NASA

Three mission specialists in a training session in the Johnson Space Center's Shuttle Mission Simulator. (SMS). From left to right: Astronauts Steven Hawley, Judith Resnik, and Richard Mullane NASA

Astronaut Resnik aboard the SMS NASA

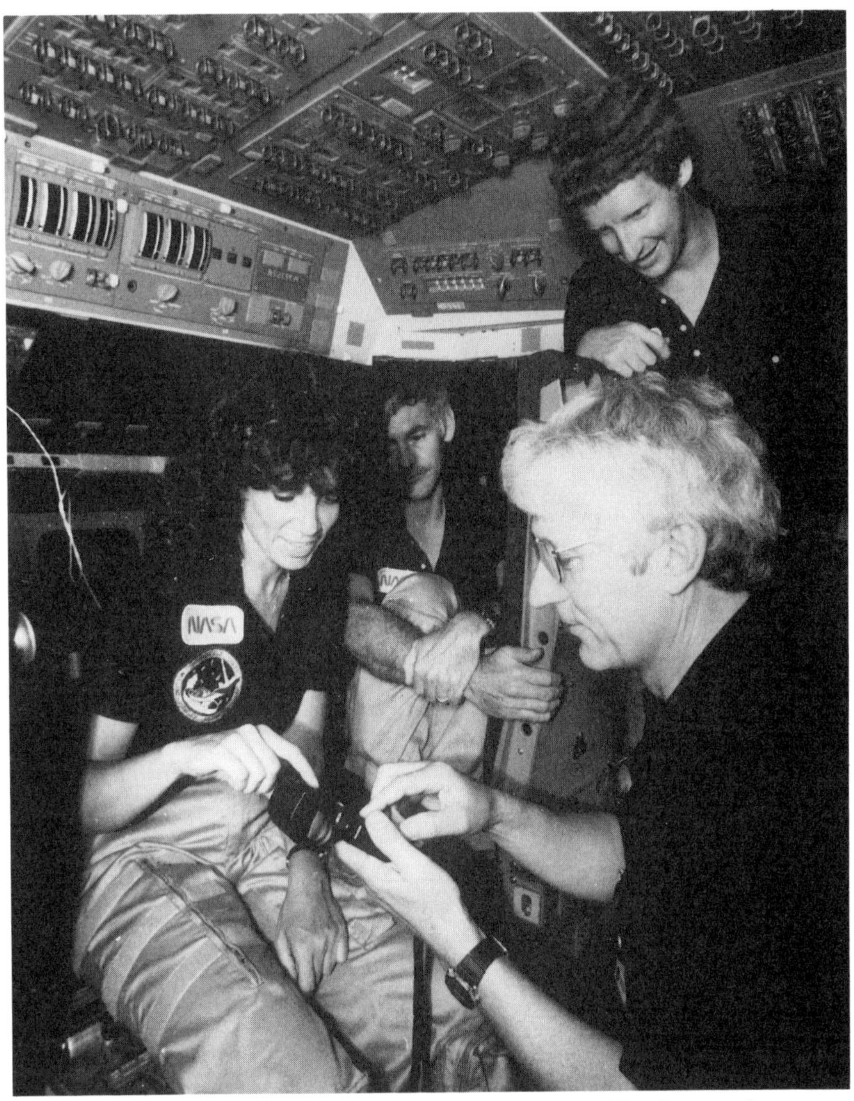

Astronauts Judith Resnik, Michael Coats, Steven Hawley, and Francis Scobee participate in a briefing session on a camera to be used in space. NASA

During a training session, mission specialist Resnik works with an experiment that she will later perform in space (left). NASA

Navy man who trained Judy in using the arm, worked with her for months that turned into years, yet he never knew she had been married and divorced or that she was Jewish. In the computerlike jargon of the space program, Harvey said, "We just didn't interface about things like that."

6
The Flight of Discovery

The most doggedly determined astronaut, male or female, ever to suit up.

—Time Magazine,
about Judith Resnik

Astronaut Judith A. Resnik was not the first woman in space. That distinction is held by Russian cosmonaut Valentina V. Tereshkova, who flew in Vostok 6, June 16–19, 1963. Nor was Judith Resnik the first American woman in space. That honor eventually went to Sally Ride, who, like Judy, joined NASA in 1978. Sally would blast off in the Challenger in June 1983. Judy became the second American woman in space, the fourth woman overall. She was, however, the first Jewish astronaut in space.

But titles and firsts meant little to J.R. She did not want to be known as the first of any group, she wanted to be known only as a scientist, an astronaut who took her job and her dedication very, very seriously.

When Judy was not named to be the first American woman in space, it was said that the reason for choosing

Sally Ride over her was the matter of publicity. NASA officials knew there would be a great deal of hoopla connected with the flight carrying the first American woman into space. They also knew that this was precisely the sort of thing that made Judy Resnik uncomfortable.

Sally Ride, in contrast, it was said, "handles the press better." Unlike Judith, Sally had always been a team player who could manage the limelight. In fact, before pursuing a doctorate in astrophysics from Stanford University, for many years Sally had imagined she was headed for a career as a professional athlete. She had become accomplished in football and softball, and was ranked nationally as a teenage tennis player. In fact, tennis star Billie Jean King had urged Sally Ride to leave Stanford to play professionally.

Sally and Judy never discussed who would be first, but talked only of the missions. To interviewers, Judy said things like, "I am just pleased to have a flight assignment. I feel that I am very fortunate to be any woman in space, any person in space."

NASA had been slow in accepting women and minorities in space. In the early years of the manned space program, in July 1961, a NASA spokesperson commented on the possibilities of including women: "Talk of an American spacewoman makes me sick to my stomach." The women's movement, the civil rights movement, and great efforts of many people changed that thinking considerably.

After nearly six years in training, Judy had truly become an astronaut. She had earned her chance in space. In late 1983, she telephoned her father from Houston to tell him that she was scheduled for a space ride the following June. "She's starting to get excited," her father said.

Judy was to be part of the crew on the maiden flight of the space shuttle Discovery. It was the fourth space plane, known as an orbiter, in the U.S. space shuttle program. The name Discovery is a familiar one in American history. The space shuttle is named for one of the tall ships, the sailing ship U.S.S. *Discovery*, which served during the American Revolution.

Before this historic mission, Dr. Marvin Resnik and his daughter went to visit Rabbi Feffer in his study at their Akron synagogue. The spiritual leader of Temple Beth El wished Judy Resnik well. He recited the traditional Jewish blessing given before a journey. "May you go in peace. May you come in peace."

The Space Shuttle Transportation System (STS), usually just known as the space shuttle, was an important step forward for the United States in space. Beginning with the first manned spacecraft in 1961, both America and the U.S.S.R. used one-shot flight containers, called ballistic reentry capsules. Each one was used for just one flight. The earliest U.S. capsules carried one astronaut (the Mercury program); then two (Gemini, beginning in 1965); and then Apollo, the three-person capsule that first landed men on the moon—American astronauts Neil Armstrong and Buzz Aldrin—in 1969.

The last flight of a U.S. ballistic reentry capsule had been in 1975, when Apollo joined up with a Soviet Soyuz capsule in space. But long before that, NASA had been seriously planning a new type of manned spacecraft—the space shuttle.

The space shuttle is a different concept. It is a true space plane, and more. Actually, it is a unique combination of rocket, spacecraft, and plane. It takes off like a rocket, orbits like a spacecraft, and comes back to earth to land gently, like an airplane. Most important it is reusable; it can go into space again and again, carrying people and materials, or payloads, to launch satellites or to build space stations.

The spacecraft that makes up the shuttle system is composed of four parts. The tallest and biggest part is the orange external fuel tank, which looks like a mammoth rocket. The only part of the system that is not reusable, it is nearly 160 feet long (or about one and a half football fields), crammed with liquid hydrogen and oxygen. Like shorter and more slender guardians flanking both sides of the external fuel tank, the white solid rocket boosters contain solid rocket fuel. All three fuel sources are needed because the heavy cabin holding the crew must be launched into orbit like a rocket. Once the solid fuel is burned up, the solid rocket boosters drop off the shuttle into the ocean below. NASA later retrieves the boosters for reuse. The external fuel tank continues to fuel the main rocket engines that are part of the shuttle space plane. Once the shuttle reaches its desired speed, the fuel tank is dropped off, but not recovered.

The main part of the system, of course, is the space plane, the orbiter. Roughly the same size as a commercial jetliner, it blasts off into space carrying the crew and payload, and returns to earth as an airplane. The orbiter's aluminum framework is covered with materials to protect it from the extreme heat it must endure upon return to the earth's atmosphere. Temperatures can reach about 1,200 degrees Fahrenheit out there!

The payload bay of the orbiter carries the materials the crew will use, such as satellites to launch. The shuttle can carry an astounding thirty tons in the cargo bay. Behind the bay are the spacecraft's three main engines. In front of the bay is the crew's cabin and flight deck. The air in the cabin is kept much like earth's atmosphere.

The first orbiter, the Enterprise, was never designed to go into space, but was to be used only for testing. So the space shuttle program truly took off on April 12, 1981, when the second of the orbiters, the Columbia, was launched on a two-day mission. This first orbital shuttle flight happened to take place on the twentieth anniversary

The Discovery crew. Left to right, seated: Richard M. Mullane; Steven A. Hawley; Henry W. Hartsfield, Jr.; Michael L. Coats. Standing: Charles D. Walker, Judith A. Resnik NASA

of Yuri Gagarin's Soviet Union mission, the first manned space flight. The third orbiter, the ill-fated Challenger, spent its first five days in space in April 1983; its second mission carried Sally Ride into space two months later.

Judith Resnik was set for the maiden flight, officially known as STS 41-D, of the Discovery, orbiter number four. Coincidentally, it was the one hundredth time human beings had flown into space from earth, from any country.

In many months of intense training for this flight, Judy found her patience sorely tested when it came time to launch. The Discovery ran into what seemed to be no end of problems.

The June 1984 target date was eagerly awaited. Five of the six crew members, who had become known as the Zoo Crew because of their exuberance, had never been up in space before. The Zoo Crew included Steven Hawley, Sally Ride's husband. Only the commander, Henry Hartsfield, had had actual space experience.

On June 26, the launch had already had a one-day delay caused by the failure of a backup navigating computer. The computer was replaced with an identical one taken from Challenger. This time, with the crew strapped into their prone positions for takeoff at 8:43 A.M. the Discovery seemed A-OK. The engines were roaring. The crew listened to the countdown. Hartsfield said, "Hang on, gang, here we go."

At T minus four seconds, there was a loud exploding sound. An engine fuel valve was malfunctioning. The alarm system, directed by a computer, went into its proper functioning. Fire was briefly seen from the back of Discovery, under the nozzle of the flawed engine. Thousands of gallons of water were hosed into the engine nozzles, quickly extinguishing the fire.

Judy had invited her loved ones to the launch. In the family VIP viewing area sat Judy's father, Len Nahmi, Len's parents, her brother, her ex-husband Michael (who, unlike Judy, had wanted to be an astronaut when a child), and her mother. According to some, her mother, who had remarried, had been invited to avoid bad publicity, but it was she who slumped in her chair as the mission was aborted, her forehead held in her hands, which were folded in a gesture of prayer.

Nearly three-quarters of an hour later, it was safe for the astronauts to come out of the shuttle. Judy came out soaking wet but unharmed. There would be no shuttle flight that day.

This was the first aborted launch for any shuttle, and only the second in the history of the U.S. manned missions.

This time, the NASA safety system came through. The fuel valve difficulty that caused the problem was detected by the safety network. Judy later told an interviewer, "I was disappointed, but I was relieved that the safety systems do work. It was unfortunate that we had to check them out. But it built a confidence in the whole system."

It took time to analyze the malfunction and make necessary repairs. On July 12, NASA announced the first two scheduled flights of the Discovery would be merged as one. Further delays brought launching into August.

August 29, and the launch was on again. No go. This time the problem, detected on August 28, was in the electronic system that would guide the booster rockets.

But August 30 was another day—take-off day. On August 30 there was but a slight delay as a private plane intruded on the intended flight path. Finally, at 8:41 A.M., Eastern Daylight Time, the Discovery lifted off perfectly from the Kennedy Space Center. It carried the heaviest payload ever in the shuttle's history, more than 47,000 pounds.

This Zoo Crew, like others before it, had added to the eventual weight by bringing sentimental trinkets aboard. Judy carried the dog tag worn by Elissa, the shaggy-haired dog who had followed her and Michael around the campus at Carnegie-Mellon. Also aboard were little surprises for one another. For Judy, the crew had hidden something in the lining of the bathroom curtain. A poster of Tom Selleck, whom Judy was known to have a crush on, was hanging so that she would see it when she entered the area. The crew

The Discovery on the launch pad

The Discovery crew about to board the shuttle (right) NASA

got the idea from a coffee cup Judy had that said, "Excuse No. 1: I'm Saving Myself for Tom Selleck." The crew members were not the only ones to bring a sense of fun to an otherwise serious venture. Mission Control woke up the astronauts one morning by playing the victory song from the University of Maryland, where Judy got her Ph.D.

Along with mission specialist Dr. Judith Resnik for the nearly seven-day flight were the commander, Henry W. Hartsfield, Jr.; the pilot, Michael L. Coats; payload specialist Charles D. Walker, an employee of McDonnell Douglas and the first such commercial specialist on a space shuttle crew; and mission specialists Steven A. Hawley and Richard M. Mullane.

The main purpose of flight STS 41-D was to deploy three satellites and to test the solar sail. The crew would also perform photography and crystal growth experiments.

Soon after they entered orbit, Dr. Judith Resnik's voice came over the shuttle radio. Said the excited astronaut, "The earth looks great!"

On this flight, Judy's specialty was the solar sail, or wing. Folded during launch into a package only about seven inches long, it was thirteen feet wide and could extend to more than one hundred feet in space. It was Judy's job to use the robot arm to raise and lower the sail several times during the mission. The main purpose was to learn how such a huge, flexible structure could be handled in space, with an eye to using it one day to capture energy from the sun for a space station. The eventual intention was for shuttle crews to be able to deliver and install solar panels such as these on space stations. These immense rectangular panels have been compared to the wings of prehistoric birds, and they are so large they would dominate the space station. Because they are constructed of extremely thin metal called gallium arsenide, it is desirable to test them in space. Flight 41-D was the first such test.

Operating the solar sail was a tricky maneuver. The sail itself was located in the open cargo bay of the shuttle, but Judy controlled it from inside the cabin, watching through a window. She reported it took nearly ten minutes to unfurl it only seventy feet.

During the launch, the wing was unfolded to its complete length of 102 feet. It was the largest structure the United States had ever erected in orbit. It was unfolded and refolded a number of times to see how durable it was and to test the solar cells on it. While the sail was unfolded, the crew also fired the vernier engines, small engines used for fine maneuvers in space. They were trying to see how the

The Discovery crew enjoying the weightless environment NASA

wing responded under the stress of vibration. The sail remained stable.

It was obvious through the television pictures coming back from space that astronaut Resnik, despite her serious manner, was thoroughly enjoying her first space flight.

Judy sent another message from space. When the Discovery was snugly in orbit, circling the earth at five miles a second, Judy held up a handwritten sign in front of the closed-circuit TV cameras on board the Discovery. The message was beamed back to earth, the message from space to Dr. Marvin Resnik. It read, "Hi Dad."

The public seemed to delight in learning tidbits about what it was like to be out of the normal world. A well-known photo from that mission shows Judy, with her mass of curly hair, floating about the cabin, demonstrating the lack of gravity. Other scenes show dehydrated packages of scrambled eggs or strawberries floating through the shuttle at dinnertime, or the astronauts looking much like mummies trying to sleep. Astronauts have sleeping bags with stiff pads to offer support, and they can sleep anywhere, floating freely in the air, or they can tie their sleeping bags onto something such as a wall or the lockers, to stay basically in one position. Judy tied her bedding to the floor. Some of the astronauts wore black sleep eye covers, which they called Lone Ranger masks, because the Discovery orbited the sun every ninety minutes or so. About half of that time, the sun shone brilliantly in.

After all the troubles with the launch, the flight of the Discovery was rather uneventful, if that word can ever be used for a space flight. The crew, however, did earn the nickname Icebusters. They were able to remove dangerous ice particles from the outside of the orbiter by using the Remote Manipulator System—the robot arm. The ability to use it may have saved their lives.

Judy sends a message to her father from the Discovery's mid-deck. NASA

Finally, after ninety-six orbits of the earth, the shuttle came home. It landed in the early morning hours of September 5, 1984, at Edwards Air Force Base in California. The young woman from Akron was now a veteran. She had 144 hours and 57 minutes logged in space.

Though Judy never relished public fusses made over her, she was most gracious to those who felt close to her, and who shared in her accomplishments. One such person was Rabbi Lerer, who wrote a letter of congratulations to his former Hebrew school student. It read:

Dear Dr. Resnik:

When you made the 7-day maiden voyage of the space shuttle Discovery, which was praised as being "perfectly accomplished," I took personal pride in this historic event. Seeing your picture caused me to reminisce over the fact that I was privileged to officiate at your Bat Mitzvah on April 6, 1962, and at your confirmation ceremony on June 7, 1964. It also inspired me to write an article for the bulletin of my synagogue, Beth Israel Community Center of Mexico City, which I transcribe here.

THE JEWISH ASTRONAUT

> The spoken word has a tremendous effect, positively or negatively, especially when it is spoken from the pulpit. The Sages, in *The Ethics of Our Fathers,* state, "Ye wise men, be heedful of your words."

Twenty-four years ago, when the penetration of space by satellites in search of widening the scope and horizon of human comprehension was very popular, this eventful phenomenon was discussed by clergymen of all denominations. Does religion approve of the search of the heights and the depths?

I delivered a sermon from my pulpit at Beth El Congregation in Akron, Ohio. I quoted the Torah which says, "Man was made in the image of God, and has been granted dominion over all creation," and, as King David in his Book of Psalms *said, "Oh God, Thou hast made Man but little less than Divine and hast crowned him with glory and honor." Yes, this is what Judaism says God has endowed Man with, a soul which is a spark of Divinity, and the capacity for tremendous achievement. Go and penetrate the heights and depths of the Universe. Penetrate space and search the planets and stars of the galaxies. Learn, seek, search, discover, and perfect creation. Consequently, this led to the achievement of the perfection of Man who is the crown of God's creation.*

. . . You undoubtedly remember that your parents were close friends of mine and I always enjoyed speaking Hebrew with your father, Dr. Marvin Resnik. Please convey my regards to them and, with personal best wishes for continued success and for a very happy Chanukah, I am,

Sincerely yours,
Rabbi Samuel S. Lerer

P.S. Because I am so proud of you, I would like to prevail upon your kindness to send me an autographed picture of yourself, to be cherished by your Rabbi. Thank you.

To this letter, Judy graciously replied, enclosing a smiling NASA photo:

Rabbi Lerer,

Thank you for your note and for remembering me from Akron. It was certainly a pleasant surprise to hear from you!

Fortunately, the years have been good to me. I am very happy with my work.

I will certainly tell my father of your letter. Best wishes to your family!

Judy Resnik

Judy's hometown also saw fit to honor its local heroine. About a month after Judy's return from her first space flight, she was honored at a gathering of family, friends, and teachers. She told the crowd she would like to be a career astronaut and stay as "long as NASA wants me." She also showed the assembled group a film of the flight, making comments about lift-off and ice problems and the fun of eating in space, which she called "dinnertime at the zoo."

Perhaps to some of those listening to Judy, it was strange that this serious, very private woman could seem so lighthearted and at ease, speaking so offhandedly before this audience. But those who knew her best surely understood. It might be that Judy had truly found her life's work. J.R. had just returned from doing what she wanted to do more than anything else in the world. She had just taken her first trip to the stars.

7

All Systems Go!

It does not enter any of our minds that we're doing something dangerous.

—*Judith Resnik*

The official press releases from NASA made space shuttle mission 51-L seem just a bit dry and routine. After listing the crew members, the release stated:

ORBITER: Challenger (009)
LAUNCH SITE: Pad 39-B, Kennedy Space Center, Fla.
LAUNCH DATE/TIME: Jan. 24, 1986—3:43 P.M. EST
ORBITAL INCLINATION: 38.45 degrees
INSERTION ORBIT: 153.5 n.mi circular
MISSION DURATION: 6 days, 34 minutes
ORBITS: 96 full orbits; landing on 97
LANDING DATE/TIME: Jan. 30, 1986, 4:17 P.M. EST

Except for the name of the orbiter and the launch site, none of the specifications ever go as planned.

But it is a long time from planning a space mission to the launch date. A lot of people and a lot of machines have to do an awful lot of work in between.

The expressed objective of this twenty-fifth shuttle flight was to launch a second Tracking and Data Relay Satellite into space. The first TDRS had been launched in 1983 on the sixth shuttle flight. Together, the two satellites were expected to provide communications coverage for about 85 percent of every orbit of a spacecraft. Also aboard the Challenger would be a science payload programmed to track the approaching Halley's comet. Named for English astronomer Edmund Halley, who first predicted its return in 1682, the comet has always fascinated scientists and amateur astronomers. Its orbit brings it into view of the earth about every seventy-six years, and scientists in 1986 expected their best look ever with the sophisticated tracking equipment aboard the Challenger.

Flight 51-L was scheduled to have two other firsts going for it. It would be the first time the shuttle was launched from pad 39-B, which had last been used in 1975 for the Apollo Soyuz (American-Russian) space project. And it would carry the first teacher into space in the person of Christa McAuliffe of Concord, New Hampshire. On August 27, 1984, President Reagan announced that a schoolteacher would be chosen as the first citizen passenger to go into space, to remind all Americans "of the crucial role teachers and education play in the life of our nation." The President added, "I can't think of a better lesson for our children, and our country." Christa McAuliffe was the finalist in a nationwide search for the best example of an American teacher.

She was scheduled to teach some lessons and provide demonstrations from space that would be beamed back to earth live and filmed for later classroom use. The first lesson, titled "The Ultimate Field Trip," would offer an insider's tour of the shuttle, from the computers and controls to the galley and bathroom. The second was called "Where We've Been, Where We're Going, and Why." In this one McAuliffe would discuss the history of aeronautics and explain the benefits of space science and why space stations are planned. One of her demonstrations would show how familiar substances such as water and oil react differently when mixed in an environment almost devoid of gravity. (They do not separate in the weightless space cabin.) Another would illustrate Newton's three laws.

J.R. was helpful to Christa and the other teachers from the start of the competition. She was part of a team sent to Washington, D.C. to give an insider's view of space to the group of teachers who won the first round of elimination contests and were now vying to be the one teacher in space.

The teachers visited the National Air and Space Museum to watch the inspiring film, *The Dream Is Alive*. The thrilling thirty-seven-minute movie, on huge screens, vividly portrays space missions. It includes scenes of Judy Resnik releasing a communications satellite into orbit and shows her eating and sleeping in space.

Then the group met astronauts in person. J.R. described Discovery mission 41-D to the mesmerized audience, including her nervousness in crossing the 150-foot-high catwalk to the shuttle, aggravated by her surprising fear of heights. She told of the intense bands of red and blue that flashed across the black horizon seconds before each of sixteen daily sunrises a crew enjoys each day, heralding the sun's arrival. For Christa McAuliffe, it was inspiring. "I felt like I was on the middeck," Christa reported. "I felt like I was flying with her. I wasn't ready to come down."

At the close of the briefing session, J.R. told the 113 teachers, "It's a shame every one of you can't be taken, because you're all real winners. I sure look forward to meeting the lucky person, and with any luck I'll still be on that mission, too."

As Christa moved along the selection and training process, although J.R. didn't really agree with the NASA decision to have nonscientists go into space, she nevertheless provided help and advice. She explained the KC-135, for example. A flight on the KC-135 jet, affectionately known as the Vomit Comet, simulates a space experience by traveling six miles high at nearly the speed of sound, then diving at a forty-five-degree angle, followed by coasting for thirty to forty-five seconds. The dive creates forces similar to the force astronauts endure during lift-off and landing. The coasting produces the weightlessness of space travel. A ride on the KC-135 is like a ride on the most frightening roller coaster, and then some.

Before the KC-135 flight, Christa was very nervous. She had just had a rocky experience in the spatial disorientation chair. This chair spins you around to simulate the dizziness you can feel in the first minutes of weightlessness. She had tried to impress the NASA instructors and prove to herself she no longer suffered from motion sickness of her childhood, but the chair was stronger than her will and she emerged from it dizzy and ill.

After the disorienting chair episode, Christa sat near Judy at lunch in the Space Center cafeteria and told her how discouraged she was. Judy reassured Christa, as she had calmed the fears of so many friends in the past. Referring to the KC-135 ride that was coming next, she said, "You know how it is, only the men get sick." J.R. also advised Christa and the other nine finalists about the preparatory medicine for the KC-135 experience. "Listen," she said. "That medicine they gave you is too strong. You'll be much more comfortable later if you only take half of it."

"It's too late," Christa and the others replied, wondering if they'd all been poisoned.

During the KC-135 ride, Judy and veteran astronaut Dale Gardner made the floating experience fun for the teacher astronaut candidates by emptying a bag of toys into the weightless environment. In their kit were paper airplanes, tennis balls, a Frisbee, a water bottle, and pieces of string. During the coasting seconds after each dive, the teachers tossed the objects around as they themselves bounced about the padded cabins of the plane. The jet dove twenty-seven times in two hours, and with each dive the teachers got better at guiding themselves about in slow motion, learning little tricks like how to cock a finger to move in a particular direction. By the end of the ride, when everyone, including Christa, was getting nauseated, the group had developed considerable skill. To celebrate their achievement, they formed a circle in midair holding hands. When they landed on earth at last, the flight crew spirited away the somewhat queasy teachers. J.R. helped them unwind over a Cajun lunch.

Eventually, the other teachers were eliminated, and Christa McAuliffe won the honor of becoming the first teacher in space. The enthusiasm of the woman who described a space adventure as "an E ticket [good for the best attractions] at Disneyland" had been infectious. All the teachers were great candidates, but of the ten finalists, she was the one who had done her homework best, who had ranked best on psychological tests, who would likely make the best presentation to large groups of people. Most important to NASA, of the finalists Christa had most clearly understood how to use the space experience to excite teachers about the space program. Christa's reaction became the headline in the *Concord Monitor:* WOW!

Challenger was also to have another first, even if NASA didn't say so. It would be the first crew to significantly represent the contributions of minorities and women. The seven-person team included two women, one black American, and one Japanese American. This professional, talented, highly trained, unusual space shuttle crew was designed to carry the American space shuttle program right into the twenty-first century.

Who were these special people who made up the crew?

All seven members of the crew did not get together at the space training center in Houston, Texas, until September 1985 when the two civilians, teacher Christa McAuliffe and electrical engineer Greg Jarvis, arrived. Of the five astronauts scheduled to board the Challenger, Judy, Francis (Dick) Scobee, Ronald McNair, and Ellison Onizuka had each been in space once before. Michael Smith was to make his first trip.

Quiet, serious Dick Scobee, the spacecraft commander, had been a space mission pilot in 1984. His experience in handling large, heavy planes made him ideal for the shuttle flights.

Mike Smith, Navy test pilot and mission pilot on the flight, was already looking forward to his second space trip because he feared he would be so excited on his first flight that he might miss something.

Ron McNair, mission specialist, was perhaps more like J.R. than any of the other crew members—private, professional, highly intelligent, and intensely motivated. His physics background was immensely important to the scheduled observations of Halley's comet. Also like Judy, he had a sense of humor. He once showed up for a photo-taking session wearing a black beret and carrying a sign that said, "Cecil B. McNair." (Cecil B. De Mille was a famous Hollywood director.) Like Judy, McNair was also a musician. He wanted to take his saxophone onboard the space mission. "You can't take your sax," Scobee had kidded, "because Judy can't take her piano."

Born in Hawaii, El Onizuka was fun loving, too, often bringing back macadamia nuts from his home state. A lieu-

The crew of the space shuttle Challenger. Left to right, seated: Michael J. Smith; Francis R. Scobee; Ronald B. McNair. Standing: Ellison S. Onizuka; Christa McAuliffe; Gregory Jarvis; Judith A. Resnik NASA

tenant colonel in the Air Force, he had logged seventy-four hours in space. Like McNair and Judy, Onizuka was a mission specialist on the flight of the Challenger. He was to help deploy the communications satellite.

As one of the three mission specalists on flight 51-L, Judy was primarily responsible for operating the shuttle's movable arm that would help put the $100 million communications satellite into orbit. She was an expert in its operation and had helped to develop the polelike robot arm.

Another of her concerns was to track and photograph Halley's comet. In the NASA Challenger insignia, worn on the left side of the astronauts' suits, was a different symbol next to each crew member's name. Halley's comet was pictured next to Judy's name, an apple-for-the-teacher rested beside Christa McAuliffe's name.

The civilians who joined this team were Greg Jarvis and Christa McAuliffe. Jarvis, payload specialist aboard the flight, was an electrical engineer and had been selected for space flight in 1984. Twice before he had been bumped off shuttle fights to make room for a senator and a congressman. Now he was ready for flight 51-L.

Christa McAuliffe, schoolteacher, wife, and mother, had received much press attention as part of the Reagan administration's spotlight on education. Her backup, Barbara Morgan, also went to Houston for training in case Christa was unable to make the flight.

This was the crew of Challenger, with its cross-section of ethnic backgrounds, representing a microcosm of American society in the 1980s. All were professionals in their way, dedicated, able, and ready for the flight of mission 51-L.

Perhaps of the seven, Judy Resnik was the most private, the most reserved, but everyone liked her. While she was the only crew member not listed in the phone book, the others realized she could and would laugh and joke with them. She joined the others at local restaurants. At Pe-Te's and Frenchie's, she allowed her picture to hang on the wall with those of other astronauts. The chef at Frenchie's knew them all, down to what they repeatedly ordered. For Judy, the order was *scallopini pescatore.*

When it came to publicity, however, they knew Judy had little time for the trappings of celebrity. Being a member of a space shuttle crew, especially this space shuttle crew, meant a lot of media attention. This flight was intended to alter the blasé attitude toward the space program Americans had developed.

Judy didn't think that exposing her private history or thoughts added anything positive to the work of being an astronaut. And it might bring something negative. Some people had flown several times, while others waited years to fly at all. Some were still waiting. Could what they said have had something to do with it? Better to say as little as possible. But sometimes Judy couldn't keep her dislike for publicity inside and it showed. Once, when asked how she felt about all the attention, she answered, "I feel like a potted plant."

From September until the winter break at the end of 1985, the Challenger crew trained intensely for the mission. They usually began training at 8 A.M., although not as a group, and continued through the day, with a break for lunch. As the days drew nearer to launch, the training became more intense, and the seven members of the team began to train as one unit.

Perhaps it was ironic that in 1985 so few people thought very much about sending a civilian schoolteacher off into space. Certainly few talked about the danger, fantasizing instead about the adventure. Most Americans had grown used to seeing rockets blasting off toward the heavens. J.R.'s Discovery mission 41-D in 1984 had been the twelfth shuttle mission. The early 1986 mission 51-L on Challenger was to be the twenty-fifth journey. To many young Americans, space flight seemed as natural as jet flight. Even more so, perhaps. After all, jets sometimes crashed. Spaceships didn't.

And then it was January 1986, and it had all come together. The crew was trained and ready and eager to go. Judy's father and stepmother, along with her brother, Chuck, and his family, would be at the Kennedy Space Center to see her glorious ride. She had actually sent Tom

Selleck a letter inviting him to the launch, but his staff had called to decline. She had also invited Mr. Nutter, her math teacher from Firestone High. She had agreed to take along into space a signet ring for her nephew and a heart-shaped locket for her niece, and a cigarette lighter from Len Nahmi.

The spacecraft Challenger was ready. The crew was ready. Judy Resnik, mission specialist was certainly ready.

All systems go!

8

The Last Flight of the Challenger

Aaall riiight!

—Judith Resnik, the first voice heard from the Challenger upon lift-off

After months of intense training and anticipation, Judy thinks that flight 51-L may never get off the ground. With the lift-off originally set for January 24, problems on the neighboring launch pad and then with the weather bring a series of delays. One of the other three space shuttles, the Columbia, has had its own delays, finally flying between January 12 and 18. These flights have begun to seem so routine that Columbia's mission draws little attention from the public and press. But three scrubs in three launch tries for the Columbia, plus the delays in landing, move the Challenger's launch date to Saturday, January 25.

On Saturday, eager Judy and the other crew members are disappointed again. Now the problem is a dust storm, not in Florida at the launch site, not even in the United States for that matter. The dust storm is near Dakar, the capital of Senegal in western Africa. Why is a storm so far

away of concern to a launch in Florida? Because an emergency landing site is located near Dakar. In accordance with NASA rules, no shuttle will be launched if something is wrong at a possible emergency landing facility.

On Sunday morning, the crew is ready once again. Now the weather problems are much closer to home. Showers are moving down the Florida coast. Unlike an airplane, the space plane will not take off in rain for fear of damage to the tiles that cover the spacecraft's thin skin.

Another delay. The launch is now set for Monday. And Monday does look better. Judy feels more confident that they will be lifting off that day. At the traditional launch breakfast for the crew, she eats two steaks and lots of scrambled eggs. Veteran space traveler Resnik is well aware that for the next several days, she is scheduled to eat vacuum-sealed flight rations. So the real thing looks especially grand at this moment.

The Challenger crew at the prelaunch breakfast NASA

A good deal of hoopla and press coverage characterize the day of a launch, especially this launch, because a teacher is on board. Publicity-shy Judy takes it with good grace. She smiles and waves along with the rest as the seven-member crew, now dressed in blue spacesuits and black boots, walk single-file to the waiting Astrovan that will take them to the launch.

Shortly before 7:30 A.M., the Astrovan drives slowly up to the waiting spacecraft on pad 39-B. Now conditions really look better, for suddenly the sun breaks out of the cloud cover. Everything is looking good.

From the van, astronauts are led into the so-called White Room, where they are helped into their harnesses and helmets. From there, one by one, they pull themselves into the hatch and climb the ladder to the flight deck. Judy is the fourth crew member to enter, behind Scobee, Smith, and Onizuka.

The Challenger orbiter has two decks for the crew, just in front of the cargo bay, where the astronauts strap into their couches for the lift-off. On the lower mid deck are Onizuka, Jarvis, and McAuliffe. On the upper flight deck, in two rows, are Commander Scobee and Pilot Smith, and behind them McNair and Judy Resnik. From their positions flat on their backs, strapped into their couches, they can see the promising blue sky. Judy waits tensely and quietly for the ride.

Then trouble, but not the weather this time. As part of the countdown to launch, the closeout team must go through a rigid schedule of checks, much as the crew of a jet plane does before takeoff. But when the team tries to remove an exterior handle on the outside hatch, they encounter a sticky bolt on a hatch. Astoundingly, this multibillion dollar operation doesn't have backup tools. When the special drill meant to open the hatch doesn't work, there isn't a second one to bring to the task. Finally, after failing to free it any other way, someone just saws it off.

The countdown has been holding all this time, of course. The Challenger crew members still lie in their couches, waiting. Now is it a go?

Unhappily for the crew and all concerned with the launch, the weather is acting up again. This time, wind gusts up to thirty-five miles an hour are sweeping around the Space Center. The wind isn't so much a problem on lift-off; but it is a safety issue again. If anything malfunctions on lift-off, Scobee or Smith could call up the RTLS, or Return to Launch Site. On command, the orbiter would be released from the booster rockets and external fuel tank. Then the spacecraft could return to the landing strip at the Space Center.

If the RTLS is necessary, winds gusting up to thirty-five miles an hour might endanger a safe landing for Challenger. NASA, attempting to ensure safety, says no to the launch once again.

Judy and the other frustrated would-be space travelers climb wearily out of their couches. They have been lying flat on their backs for five and a half hours.

Flight 51-L is now scheduled for Tuesday, January 28, 1986. Launch time is initially set for 9:38 A.M., later changed to 10:38 A.M., and finally to 11:38 A.M.

Blue sky greets the blue-clad crew as once more they head for the launch pad in the cold Florida air. And cold it is. Just before dawn on Tuesday morning, although the winds have died down, the temperature has fallen to twenty-seven degrees Fahrenheit. This is most unusual for Florida. And the temperature is very significant because the bottom limit for launching flight 51-L is twenty-eight degrees F.

The astronauts awake at 6:20 A.M. and get together for breakfast. They're pleased with the white-frosted cake NASA bakers have prepared, decorated lavishly with their names, the crew emblem, and a picture of the Challenger itself.

By 7:20 they are being briefed on conditions. They are hopeful.

Strapped in their couches once more, aware of the problems concerning the temperature, Judy and the others joke about the weather and try not to think about another aborted mission. When they had entered the White Room earlier that morning, Judy, clapping her hands in the cold air, had told Christa McAuliffe, who would be strapped in a deck below, that the next time they saw each other, they would be in space.

In the meantime, families and friends of the Challenger crew, including Judy's father, stepmother, and brother and his family, are celebrating in anticipation in Launch Control

Francis Scobee and Judith Resnik lead the way onto the Challenger.
NASA

Center, four miles from pad 39-B. Mr. Nutter, the math teacher, who had been there earlier for an aborted launch, has had to return home. Other spectators, thousands of motorists in the Space Center area, all staring skyward, wait impatiently for the launch. And all across the country, millions of viewers sit before their television sets . . . waiting for another exciting, if almost commonplace lift-off of the shuttle.

By 9 A.M. the Challenger crew is sealed inside the space shuttle waiting for the final decision. Impatient and anxious to go, they nonetheless somewhat expect another mission abort because of the intense cold. "I hope we don't drive this down to the bitter end again today," Judy says.

Engineers for Morton Thiokol, manufacturers of key shuttle parts, watching conditions, warn that the cold temperature could cause the O-rings in the rocket boosters to become less resilient, allowing explosive gases to leak through. There is a lot of pressure to get this launch up. The administrators above those cautioning engineers get the final say and they declare that the system will function.

At 9:08 the countdown is halted suddenly. Rocco Petrone, the president of Rockwell Space Transportation Systems, builder of the shuttle, is concerned about the icicles on the launch pad. He calls NASA to warn against launching. The decision is made to launch anyway, because the wind has died down and the NASA ice inspection team has carefully gone over the shuttle numerous times. The ice team decides that the icicles that have formed on the craft pose little or no danger and will break away at lift-off.

Mission Control contacts Commander Scobee in the Challenger. Countdown resumes. The launch time is now set for 11:38.

The countdown begins again as the Challenger's main computer (which has four backups in case of failure) continuously searches the entire shuttle system looking for problems. None is found.

T minus seven minutes and counting. With the Challenger detached from its walkway, the shuttle stands poised on the launch pad. It is now connected only to the external fuel tank, carrying more than 143,000 gallons of liquid oxygen and 385,000 gallons of liquid hydrogen, and two boosters, each stuffed with more than 1 million pounds of solid fuel. The liquid oxygen and hydrogen are connected by lines to the shuttle, where they will mix and drive the Challenger's engines. The solid fuel in the boosters will ignite upon lift-off and burn completely.

T minus six minutes and counting. Pilot Smith reaches over and turns on the auxilliary power units.

T minus four minutes and counting. "Visors down," orders Commander Scobee. Judy and the others close the airtight visors on their helmets.

T minus three minutes and counting. The Challenger is now operating on its own electrical power.

T minus two minutes . . . looking good. T minus ninety seconds . . . "The 51-L mission ready to go," says Mission Control to a relieved and expectant crew. T minus forty-five seconds. Streams of water gush out around the spacecraft to dampen the sound level when the Challenger lifts off. Otherwise, the noise from the engines will be so great it could actually damage the spacecraft.

As spectators hold their breath in anticipation, the crew is silent inside the ship. As if from a distance, they can hear the whirring of the Challenger's mechanisms as it prepares for the tremendous shock of lift-off.

And now the computers take over the firing sequence of the main engines. The launch can still be aborted, but it is out of the astronauts' hands.

T minus six seconds . . . "We have main engine start," says the calm voice of Mission Control. The instrument panels of the Challenger are ablaze with blinking lights, and a whining vibration signals the startup of the three main engines. As each engine reaches its full thrust, the vibration turns into a great surging roar that screams into the tightly visored space helmets.

Three . . . two . . . one . . . lift-off of the spacecraft Challenger!

Judy, who has been the most joking and outgoing of the crew members this morning, shouts "Aaall riiight!" as the shuttle leaps off the space pad in a cloud of steam and fire. As spectators cheer and television viewers ooh and aah at the spectacle, the screaming orbiter blasts toward the heavens with a roar that deafens the ears.

Inside the Challenger, strapped to their couches, their heads rattling around in their space helmets, the crew can hardly hear the voice of Mission Control. They know full well that this is the most dangerous part of their space mission. Judy and the others are jammed back against their seats with three times the force of gravity. The situation for them at this moment is not in their control. This time when they have no control is the time, the only time, that Judy Resnik feels there might be danger.

If Judy and the crew can hardly hear Mission Control, the spectators can't, either. Onlookers shout with delight and awe as the space shuttle blasts skyward at an unbelievable rate of speed and noise level. Reporters later will say they do not remember so strong a noise level on earlier missions. And tracking cameras will later show that at 0.4 seconds after lift-off, black smoke is emerging from the lower end of the right solid booster. The smoke is seen for the first twelve seconds of the flight.

Sixteen seconds into the flight of the Challenger . . . "Houston, we have roll program," says Commander Scobee, as the space shuttle, clinging like a bug to the fuel tank, turns with precision onto its back. "Looks like we've

The Challenger lifts off on January 28, 1986, at 11:38 A.M. NASA

got a lot of wind here today," comments Pilot Smith as the crew experiences the first stiff winds to buffet the spacecraft. The Challenger sways and shudders under the tremendous force. It has now reached 10,000 feet and is traveling at half the speed of sound.

Thirty-five seconds into the flight of the Challenger . . . The three main engines are throttled down to 65 percent of their power. Everything is running normally, everything looks good.

Forty seconds into the flight, at 19,000 feet, Challenger tears through the sound barrier.

Fifty-two seconds into the flight. "Go with throttle up." This means that the engines automatically have reached full power, and systems are go. In a matter of seconds, Scobee confirms throttle up. The spacecraft and crew will now face their greatest stress.

But disaster is already in the making, and a combination of factors seals the fate of the Challenger. For one thing, the ship slams into the most violent winds ever encountered on a space shuttle mission. And there is fire. Undetected by all the computer systems, by the crew of the Challenger, by the experts of NASA who are monitoring the flight, or by the spectators watching from below, at 58.7 seconds, the black smoke appears again, followed by a small orange plume erupting from a joint on the righthand rocket booster. But the great heat within the booster has created a seal over the break. Perhaps without the violent winds, the seal would have held . . . perhaps . . .

But the seal does not hold. When, at 59.2 seconds, the intense flame burns through the O-ring seal and it fails, heat at over 5,000 degrees begins to escape from the broken joint. The crew does not yet know what is happening. But the NASA officials watch as, within three seconds, the tiny orange flame becomes a monstrous blowtorch.

At 60.16 seconds, the chamber pressure of the rocket booster falls.

By 66.17 seconds, the flame has migrated. Bright spots of fire are detected on top of the booster.

At 72.20 seconds, the lower end of the rocket booster breaks away and swings out from the huge external fuel tank. The top of the booster moves inward, toward the tank, rupturing it.

At 73.175 seconds, a large cloud of oxygen or hydrogen gas fuel streams from the external tank.

At 73.200 seconds, a flash fire appears between the upper part of the external fuel tank and the forward position of the Challenger.

At 73.226 seconds, the external tank's liquid fuels ignite and trigger a powerful explosion.

What is over in seconds for those on the ground may seem very much longer to those inside the space cabin. Just before the force of the explosion blows the cabin carrying the seven-member crew away from the rest of the orbiter, Pilot Mike Smith acknowledges the terrifying sight outside his window with the words "Uh, oh!"

At more than nine miles high above the Atlantic Ocean, all the worst fears of safety-conscious NASA are coming true.

In seventy-three disastrous seconds, the final Challenger flight that began with hope has ended with a tragic explosion.

The force of the explosion did not kill, and probably did not seriously injure, any of the astronauts, because the crew cabin had separated from the rest of the ship. From recovered gauges, NASA was able to determine that at least one of the Challenger crew had been breathing from an emergency air pack for several minutes. Once the cabin fell away from the rest of the ship, the only available air was in

The Challenger explosion NASA

the cabin itself and in the emergency packs. Although Scobee's emergency pack had not been turned on, Smith's was, probably by McNair or by Judy, who was strapped in behind Smith.

Whether Judy Resnik, or any other member of the Challenger crew, lived long enough to understand that a disaster was taking place, we will never know. After the explosion, hundreds of fiery spaceship pieces came tumbling down from the sky, white streamers following the flames. The fragments, including the crew compartment, fell for nearly half an hour. The cabin hit the ocean traveling at 207 miles an hour. No one knows if the crew was dead or alive upon impact, but they probably were not conscious. The human body could not survive the 200G impact of this crash. The last flight of the Challenger—after all the months of training, after all the work and dedication, after all the dreams and hopes—had taken less than two minutes.

As NASA officials slowly began to comprehend the tragedy that had occurred, most of the spectators at the Space Center stood in bewilderment. Television viewers stared in confusion, as they heard the voice of Mission Control calmly understate, "Obviously a major malfunction."

Throughout that day and the days that followed, television viewers watched and watched again the explosion, viewing and re-viewing with horror the expressions on the spectators' faces, then watching as they dejectedly filed from the viewing stands. As they stayed glued to their television sets, the American people tried to comprehend the incomprehensible.

Around the nation, people reacted with shock and sorrow. The seven crew members of the Challenger represented a cross-section of American life. Witnessing the explosion was like having a piece of the United States blown to bits. President Ronald Reagan was in the Oval Office when officials burst in to tell him the news. He later delivered a televised tribute to the Challenger crew.

Perhaps it was the schoolchildren who were most confused by the tragedy. The classmates of Christa McAuliffe's son, Scott, who were watching from the Kennedy Space Center, did not understand the disaster immediately. But when they saw the horror in the eyes and the actions of the adults, they began to cry. In many classrooms all over the country, where television monitors had been set up to view the flight, school was closed for the rest of the day. Counseling services were set up for those who needed help in coming to terms with the tragedy, or who just needed to talk about what had happened.

9
Aftershock

> There is no better way to celebrate her life than to celebrate the cause for which she gave it.
>
> —*Senator John Glenn*

In the first few moments following the terrible explosion on board the Challenger, no one on the ground could quite believe or understand what had happened. NASA technicians stared at their monitoring screens. All they saw was a series of S's; this meant no data was coming from the shuttle.

Few of the spectators watching outside realized the tragedy at first. The flames coming from the doomed spacecraft were, after all, so far away. To some of the viewers, what they saw seemed to be part of the natural separation of the shuttle from the boosters.

Judy's father and stepmother watched the lift-off from the roof of the NASA control building. This was a special viewing area set aside for family and friends of the astronauts. Dr. Resnik relaxed a little bit after the shuttle lifted off and cleared the tower. He was well aware that the few seconds after the launch are the most dangerous part of the mission.

Then he heard the explosion.

Not believing, and not wanting to believe, Dr. Resnik stared at the billowing cloud coming from the Challenger. He was waiting for the spaceship to come through the cloud and reappear. In a few seconds, he realized there was nothing at all.

Almost immediately, those people in the special viewing area were taken inside the building to what is called the ready room. But, of course, it was too late to keep them from seeing what had happened to the ones they loved.

"It was over so fast, everyone saw everything," commented Dr. Resnik.

The next day, Judy's father was back home in Ohio, where tributes honoring his daughter began.

At Temple Israel in Akron, three days after the tragedy, hundreds of people attended a memorial service for Judy. Among them were twenty NASA astronauts. Rabbi David Horowitz said of her, "She braved the terrors of the unknown for truth that shed light upon our way."

Rabbi Abraham Feffer of Temple Beth El, where Judy had her Bat Mitzvah, called her "brilliant, sensitive, and compassionate." He spoke of her visit to his office in 1984 before her first flight into space, how he'd blessed her then. Rabbi Feffer also spoke about Judy Resnik and her religion. He noted that she called her father Abba and her grandmother Bubbie, the first a Hebrew word, the second Yiddish. She could not be "too far from our people," he remarked. And although her attendance at synagogue might have been irregular, he praised Judy's quality of integrity and commitment to truth.

The governor of Ohio, Richard Celeste, also spoke at the service. He told Judy's family and friends, "She knew she would be at home in space. And she was. And she is."

All through the service honoring his daughter, Dr. Marvin Resnik, sitting between his wife and his son, listened intently. A few rows behind them sat Judy's mother, her head at times bowed in grief.

At the end of the ceremony, the cantor chanted the El Moleh Rachamin, the traditional Hebrew prayer for the dead, which brought tears to the eyes of many family members, including Bubbie, Judy's beloved ninety-two-year-old grandmother. Bubbie Anna's first reaction upon hearing Judy was going into space in 1984 seemed especially apropos now. Anna Resnik, speaking mostly in Yiddish, had said she understood that Judy was going into space, but she didn't understand why she would want to.

The service for Judy in Akron was followed by another, this one in Cleveland, where former astronaut John Glenn spoke. "In my judgment," he said, "there is no better way to celebrate her life than to celebrate the cause for which she gave it." He continued, "I hope we never forget that the words 'Go at throttle up' are far more than a courageous epitaph. They are America's destiny. And they will turn tragedy into triumph once again. Judy would be the very first to say 'fix it and let's get on with it.' "

Dr. Marvin Resnik read a condolence note from a friend, echoing the sentiments of Senator Glenn. "The Challenger is gone. But not the challenge."

And Judy's home state decided to remember her in other ways, as well. The state legislature voted to start the Judith Resnik Legislative Scholarship Program. It would allow money donations to be channeled into different scholarships for deserving students.

Other suggestions to remember Judy came pouring in from all over the state, from naming a bridge or a street for her to creating a bronze sculpture and establishing a music scholarship in her name.

Judy's picture hangs on the Firestone Wall of Fame, and her high school also boasts a Judy Resnik scholarship fund set up by the Akron Board of Education. The fund has drawn donors nationally and internationally. Judy's alma mater, Carnegie-Mellon, and the University of Maryland from which she earned her doctorate, have similar scholarships, as does Ohio State University, Dr. Marvin Resnik's school.

A hands-on replica of the Challenger, geared to children, is planned by NASA. Youngsters will be able to touch and climb on the model when they visit Houston.

An illuminated manuscript dedicated to Judith Resnik, the first Jewish astronaut, one of twenty illustrations of Hebrew text by Dorrie Schlesinger, has been on view at New York's Hebrew Union College-Jewish Institute of Religion.

In addition, there is a Judith A. Resnik B'nai B'rith Women's Chapter in Scottsdale, Arizona. Said Judy Leeds, chairperson, "We named the chapter for Judy, who was a member of the Southview Chapter of B'nai B'rith Women in Los Angeles, because we felt that she was an example of a young Jewish woman with goals and ambitions." The chapter funds the Children's Home in Israel, dedicated to helping youngsters with severe problems.

Far away in Jerusalem, plans are under way to keep Judy's memory alive. A living memorial is proposed to honor her and the rest of the Challenger crew. The plans call for a rehabilitative gym to be built in the Beit Halohem Center for Disabled Veterans in Jerusalem. Senator Glenn, a member of the committee, said that "the memory of Judith Resnik and her fellow crew members . . . will never die . . . it is fitting that homage to them be in the form of a 'living' memorial." Judy's father is honorary chairman of the memorial committee.

Even as far away as Moscow, the Challenger was hon-

The remains of the Challenger crew were moved from the Kennedy Space Center by a military honor guard. NASA

ored. "We partake of your grief at the tragic death of the crew of the space shuttle Challenger," said Soviet leader Mikhail Gorbachev in a message to President Reagan.

Back home at the Kennedy Space Center, employees also paid tribute to Judy and the Challenger crew. During a memorial service, a helicopter carried out to sea a wreath of white chrysanthemums with seven red carnations and dropped the flowers into the churning water.

Judith A. Resnik lived only thirty-six years, and her death was tragic. But she died doing a job she loved, and that thought may help those who knew her and loved her to cope with their grief. Judy wanted to reach the stars. The happiest day of her life was the day she was accepted into the space program.

An obituary for Judy in the *Jewish Press*, February 28, 1986, said: "Judith dreamt of taking a trip to another world. She wanted to experience things she had never seen or experienced before . . . We pray to Hashem [God] that there will never be any more explosions in the skies of Florida."

"They slipped the surly bonds of earth to touch the face of God." A composite of the Challenger crew NASA

"She died doing what she loved to do," said Dr. Marvin Resnik. And he also said, "The last time I saw her, we were running on the beach. I was chasing her, she was chasing me. That was the day before the launch. I prefer to remember her that way—barefoot on the sand on the beach of Cape Canaveral."

Dr. Resnik has his memories, the nation has its memories. Everyone can picture the eager, spirited young woman walking toward the spacecraft with a spring in her step as she leads the way.

10

The Dream Is Alive

The decision to launch the Challenger was flawed.

—Presidential Commission on the Space Shuttle Challenger Accident

Following the Challenger disaster, President Reagan made a pledge to Judy's father, Dr. Marvin Resnik. The President assured him that the United States would never forsake its commitment to space travel and exploration. Judy's sacrifice will not have been in vain if that commitment goes forward.

Regardless of the president's pledge, many reports appeared questioning whether NASA had acted judiciously, not only on January 28, but at other times as well. Many asked if manned flight is necessary or desirable, if the possible benefits of such programs are worth the expense, both in money and human lives. The administration and goals of the entire space program came under intense scrutiny. Its future was in question.

On June 9, 1986, less than six months after the tragedy, the Presidential Commission on the Space Shuttle Challenger Accident issued findings concerning the cause of the disaster. In brief, this is what the commission reported:

The cause of the accident was failure of a joint in the right solid rocket booster, specifically the seals. As a result, hot gases were allowed to escape and destroy the space shuttle.

Why did the joint fail? The commission concluded that NASA had followed the correct procedures in installing the joints and seals. However, it also concluded that the joint design itself was faulty and the design not fully understood by all those concerned with the launch of the shuttle. Specifically, the commission said, "The decision to launch the Challenger was flawed." It said those who made the decision to launch did not have a clear understanding of what part the extremely cold temperatures would play in the performance of the joint and seals.

The commission made another important statement. As a group, the commission was troubled because it seemed as though the desire to get the shuttle and its payload into space had repeatedly superseded the need for safety. It seemed that both NASA and Morton Thiokol had long been aware of problems with the O-rings. In post-flight inspections, about a dozen cases of hot gases reaching the primary O-rings had been noted. The worst case had been in a 1985 flight, when a secondary O-ring had also shown the eroding effect of heat. Interestingly, this flight was launched in the coldest weather prior to the Challenger tragedy.

NASA and Morton Thiokol studied and discussed the problem, but they did little. Concern at Thiokol grew, with one memo they sent to NASA starting off "Help!"—yet flight after flight took off and the problem remained unsolved. NASA and Morton Thiokol relied instead on the record of safe launchings and landings. In the report, commissioner Richard Feynman, a Nobel Prize-winning physicist characterized this type of decision making as "a kind of Russian roulette . . . the shuttle flies . . . and nothing happens. Then it is suggested, therefore, that the risk is no longer so high for the next flights. We can lower our standards a little bit because we got away with it last time."

The decision to launch Challenger had come about through a series of misguided, unclear communications, the report announced. One example occurred the day before the actual launch, on January 27. During a teleconference between bigwigs at Thiokol and NASA, Robert Lund, vice-president of engineering at Thiokol, recommended launch delay until the temperature reached fifty-three degrees Fahrenheit. A response from NASA saying, "My God, Thiokol, when do you want me to launch, next April?" led to pressure on Thiokol, though NASA said that the comment had been taken out of context. At this point, the lower level Thiokol engineers still wanted to delay the launch. Upper management at Thiokol felt pressure, rightly or wrongly, from NASA that it must prove beyond a shadow of a doubt that it was not safe to launch. During this crucial teleconference and the communications that followed it, somehow the usual thinking about safety got turned around. Thiokol tried to find some way to prove that it wouldn't work, and was unable to do that. This strange turnabout was a total reverse of the usual preflight safety check, in which everything had to be proven safe, not unsafe.

The commission reported its findings, then went on to make recommendations. The commission recommended that the joints in question be redesigned and truly fixed; that astronauts be encouraged to enter management positions in which their space flight experience and appreciation of the need for extreme safety would be most useful; that communications between branches of NASA be improved; that NASA and its contractors review all hazardous items and identify those needing fixing before the shuttle could fly again; that landing safety be improved; that maintenance safeguards be established to prevent "cannibalizing" one orbiter to provide parts for another and to ensure that inspection plans are followed strictly; and that efforts be made to design an escape system for the crew.

As a concluding thought, the commission said that it "applauds NASA's spectacular achievements of the past and anticipates impressive achievements to come. The findings and recommendations presented in this report are intended to contribute to the future NASA successes that the nation both expects and requires as the twenty-first century approaches."

The commission members were not alone in commenting on the organization and administration of NASA. Reginald Turnell, editor of *Jane's Spaceflight Directory*, has criticized the "disarray" in the U.S. space program. Dr. Sally Ride, the first American woman in space, has left the space program and taken NASA to task for its lack of clear-cut goals. Some say the space program should shoot for a lunar station on the moon. Others say it should aim for Mars.

Nevertheless, the program moves forward. A new unit is in training; among them is the first black woman astronaut, Dr. Mae Jamison, who holds a bachelor's degree in chemical engineering from Stanford University and a medical degree from Cornell. Said Dr. Jamison, "If I am a role model, I hope it will be for those who want to do something different."

Dr. Jamison continues the tradition of Judy Resnik, reminding young people of all backgrounds and heritages that they can indeed "do something different," that the barriers are coming down.

In the wake of the tragedy and the commission's findings, NASA aimed toward putting into space a safer shuttle, no matter how long that mission would take. They have narrowed their goals, no longer taking up commercial payloads. Rear Admiral Richard Truly, astronaut and head of the Naval Space Command, has set up a strategy for safely returning the space shuttle to flight status. The shuttle has been thoroughly reviewed and the rocket joint completely redesigned. James Fletcher, former NASA administrator, has been called back into service. An astronaut's wish list, composed of the ideal changes, has been drawn up. On the wish list is an escape chute.

Scores of modifications have been made, all to try to prevent a repeat of the Challenger tragedy. The nose wheel steering system has been improved to handle more easily in crosswinds during landing. A latch has been added to the main fuel valve to help avoid an accidental shutoff. Axles have been thickened and brakes made more powerful for safer landings. The number of O-rings has been increased from two to three. Wings have been strengthened for greater safety on ascent. In all, there are more than four hundred design changes in the shuttle.

At last, after many tests and as many delays, on Thursday, September 29, 1988, the command "go at throttle up" was heard once again. Ironically, the orbiter Discovery, the same shuttle that carried Judy on her memorable trip into space in 1984, was chosen for the first launch since her death. Astronauts Frederick Hauck, Richard Covey, David Hilmers, George Nelson, and John Lounge boarded the craft. Two had flown twice in space, the others once.

The world held its breath. The launch was smooth, the mission was accomplished. The shuttle was back in space.

Buoyed with renewed rigor, NASA scheduled five flights for 1989, and eight are planned for 1990. They plan to build a new shuttle, replacing Challenger and bringing the number of shuttle orbiters back to four. The new shuttle will be built at a cost of $2 billion to $3 billion, but the plan is to build slowly and carefully, over a period of seven years. NASA has already launched the Magellan satellite to orbit Venus and the Galileo probe to Jupiter's atmosphere. Other possible plans include a manned space station on the moon and the Hubble space telescope.

A manned U.S. space station is included in the vision of the future. A shuttle would go back and forth from earth to the space station, which would act as a way station to Mars. The shuttle would connect with a rocket serving as an express flight to the next planet.

The dates are uncertain. But NASA has long-range plans. The space program is moving ahead. The dream is alive. Next stop, Mars.

SUGGESTED READING

Apfel, Necia H. *Space Law*. New York: Watts, 1988.

———. *Space Station*. New York: Watts, 1987.

Atkinson, Stuart. *Journey into Space*. New York: Viking Kestrel, 1988.

Billings, Charlene W. *Christa McAuliffe: Pioneer Space Teacher*. Hillside, N.J.: Enslow, 1986.

———. *Space Station: Bold New Step Beyond Earth*. New York: Dodd, Mead, 1986.

Branley, Franklyn M. *From Sputnik to Space Shuttles: Into the New Space Age*. New York: Crowell, 1986.

———. *Mysteries of Life on Earth and Beyond*. New York: Lodestar, 1987.

Briggs, Carole S. *Women in Space: Reaching the Last Frontier*. Minneapolis: Lerner, 1987.

Clendinen, Dudley. *A Path to the Stars: The Story of Challenger V Astronaut Ron McNair*. New York: Knopf, 1986.

Cohen, Daniel, and Cohen, Susan. *Heroes of the Challenger*. New York: Archway, 1986.

Collins, Michael. *Flying to the Moon and Other Strange Places*. New York: Farrar, Straus and Giroux, 1976.

Crocker, Chris. *Great American Astronauts*. New York: Watts, 1986.

Cross, Wilbur. *Space Shuttle*. Chicago: Children's, 1985.

Dolan, Edward F. *Famous Firsts in Space*. New York: Cobblehill, 1989.

Dwiggins, Don. *Flying the Space Shuttles*. New York: Dodd, Mead, 1985.

Fichter, George S. *The Space Shuttle*. Rev. ed. New York: Watts, 1981.

Fox, Mary Virginia. *Women Astronauts Aboard the Shuttle*. Rev. ed. New York: Messner, 1987.

Furniss, Tim. *The Story of the Space Shuttle*. London: Hodder and Stoughton, 1986.

Haskins, Jim and Benson, Kathleen. *Space Challenger: The Story of Guion Bluford*. Minneapolis: Carolrhoda, 1984.

Hawkes, Nigel. *Space Shuttle*. New York: Watts, 1983.

Herder, D. J. *Research Satellites*. New York: Watts, 1987.

Hiller, B. B. and Hiller, Neil W. *Space Camp: A Novelization*. New York: Scholastic, 1986.

Joels, Kerry. *The Official Young Astronaut Handbook*. New York: Bantam, 1987.

Lampton, Christopher. *Rocketry: From Goddard to Space Travel*. New York: Watts, 1988.

McCarter, James. *The Space Shuttle Disaster*. New York: Watts, 1988.

Newton, David E. *U.S. and Soviet Space Programs: A Comparison*. New York: Watts, 1988.

O'Connor, Karen. *Sally Ride and the New Astronauts: Scientists in Space*. New York: Watts, 1983.

Olesky, Walter. *It's Women's Work Too*. New York: Messner, 1980.

Pogue, William R. *How Do You Go to the Bathroom in Space: All the Answers to All the Questions You Have About Living in Space*. New York: Doherty, 1985.

Poynter, Margaret, and Lane, Arthur L. *Voyager: The Story of a Space Mission*. New York: Atheneum, 1981.

Rickard, Graham. *Homes in Space*. Minneapolis: Lerner, 1989.

Ride, Sally, with Okie, Susan. *To Space and Back*. New York: Lothrop, Lee and Shepard, 1986.

Schulke, Flip, et al. *Your Future in Space: The U.S. Space Camp Training Program*. New York: Crown, 1987.

Shayler, David. *Shuttle Challenger: A Complete History of Space Shuttle Orbiter OV-O99*. Englewood Cliffs, N.J.: Prentice-Hall, 1987.

Smith, Carter. *One Giant Leap for Mankind*. New York: Silver-Burdett, 1986.

Smith, Howard E. *Daring the Unknown: A History of NASA*. San Diego: Gulliver, 1987.

Stoff, Joshua. *The Voyage of the Ruslan: The First Manned Exploration of Mars*. New York: Atheneum, 1986.

Taylor, L. B., Jr. *Space: Battleground of the Future?* New York: Watts, 1988.

Vogt, Gregory. *Space Shuttle: Projects for Young Scientists*. New York: Watts, 1983.

INDEX

ABOUT THE AUTHORS

JOANNE E. BERNSTEIN has written over twenty books for young readers, including *Loss: And How to Cope with It.* Of this biography she notes, "We wrote this book because we were touched by Judith Resnik's story as reported after the Challenger disaster. We thought it was important for young people to have an opportunity to learn about the first Jewish astronaut."

Ms. Bernstein lives in Brooklyn, New York.

ROSE BLUE is the author of over thirty books for young people, including *My Mother, the Witch* and *Grandma Didn't Wave Back,* which were both made into NBC Afterschool Specials. *Cold Rain on the Water* was named a Children's Book Council Notable Book.

Ms. Blue lives in Brooklyn, New York.

ALAN JAY GERBER hopes that his research for this book will help "to establish a permanent memorial in literature to Dr. Judith Resnik." He teaches English and is active in religious and civic affairs in New York City. He lives in Brooklyn, New York.